A QUAINT TOWN

FOR A KILLING

A P.G. MYSTERY BY
JEFFREY WHITMORE

PACIFIC GROVE BOOKS
Pacific Grove, California

A QUAINT TOWN FOR A KILLING
A P.G. Mystery by Jeffrey Whitmore

First Edition 2018
Updated 2019
Copyright © Jeffrey Whitmore

Cover photo: Roka

ISBN: 978-1-943887-74-3 PRINT
ISBN: 978-1-943887-75-0 EBOOK

PUBLISHED by
PACIFIC GROVE BOOKS
an Imprint of Park Place Publications
Pacific Grove, California 93950

Printed in the United States of America

OTHER BOOKS BY PACIFIC GROVE BOOKS AND KEEPERS OF OUR CULTURE:
Life in Pacific Grove, California, Book 1 (2017) and Book 2, (2018)
Pacific Grove 1974, Bill Minor, reprint 2018.

A DONATION IS MADE TO THE PACIFIC GROVE PUBLIC LIBRARY FOR EVERY BOOK PURCHASED.

"Mommy?"

The little boy in the red bathing suit stood with the heels of his rubber flip-flops resting on the sand, the toes on the edge of a beach towel.

The woman on the beach towel ignored him.

He rose up on his toes and sank back on his heels. The flip-flops made a squishing sound.

"*Mom-my!*"

She didn't look up from her paperback. "Oh god, Kevin, what is it now?"

"I saw a ghost man."

She raised her head. "Huh?"

He looked over his shoulder toward a group of boulders at the far end of the beach. "A ghost man. Behind the big rock."

"What do you mean?"

"He doesn't have a face."

She turned back to the book. "Run off and play, Kevin. Mommy wants to read."

"No."

She looked up again.

Tears trickled down the boy's cheeks. "I'm afraid," he said.

She turned toward the boulders. The largest stood about ten-feet high, an oblong granite hulk, dark gray, except at its ridge, which was whitened by gull droppings. If you had a lively imagination you could see it as a snow-capped elephant. About a third of its length—the front of the elephant, where a groove in the rock outlined the trunk—extended into the water.

She set her book down on the sand, stood up, and offered her hand to the boy. "I'll go down there with you."

He shook his head and stepped back from her, his lower lip protruding.

She sighed. "Okay, Kevin, I'll go by myself."

God, he could be exasperating. A terrific kid most of the time, but why did he have to act like such a sissy? Good thing his father wasn't here. She stepped off the towel and scooted across the hot sand to the water's edge. It was just shy of two o'clock, and the temperature had been in the high eighties since noon.

She followed the shoreline, keeping to the wet sand at the water's edge until she came to the boulder. The stack of rocks behind the boulder had to be blistering hot. She decided to wade around it. The drop-off was steep, and after a few steps she was in up to her knees. Halfway around the rock, she sniffed the air and made a face. Rotten kelp?

She was hip deep in the water when she saw the man in the black neoprene wetsuit. He lay on his back, half in and half out of the water.

She wheeled about and headed back the way she'd come. She plunged through the water, her heart pounding. She felt she was moving in slow motion. From deep within her, a scream began to rise.

Kevin had been right. Because of crabs and other nibbling things of the sea, the man had no face.

CHAPTER 1

I flung off the covers and stumbled toward the living room, yanked from sleep by the jangling telephone. Nine in the morning. God, I hate early birds. By the time I picked it up I was almost awake. I guessed who was calling.

"Presto here," I said. "Morning, Stan."

"Mr. Kane?" a woman's voice said.

I didn't recognize it. I'd assumed it was Stan Gibbs calling. He'd been badgering me about the copy I was writing for one of his ad agency clients. The deadline was a week off, but Stan likes to keep on top of the situation.

"This is he," I said to the unknown woman.

"I'm Nadine Stoughton," she said. "From Boston."

I'd never heard of her. I said, "Ah," and left it at that.

"Mr. Allred at Allred Investigations and Security recommended you for a project I'm involved in. I know it's short notice, but he said you might be able to help me."

"I'll try," I said. "What do you have in mind?"

My business cards say "Preston Kane: Writing, Editing, Creative Services." I've been a reporter, columnist, and copy editor for newspapers and magazines. Now my day job is freelance writing and editing: articles, interviews, advertising, résumés, brochures, ghost writing, grant writing—that kind of stuff.

The "creative services" bit encompasses anything else I can do to make money—so long as it's legal. I got the idea from the business card of an ex-con friend who wasn't so picky about the legality angle. He once told me his creative services were "all inclusive."

I've tended bar from time to time in the Monterey area, driven a taxi here, and for half a year managed a guided-tour service for visitors to the Central Coast.

So I wasn't thrown off my game when Nadine Stoughton said, "I'd like you to do some publicity work for me and also a bit of investigating."

It was in my ballpark. I wasn't a licensed PI, but Nick Allred had sent me out on a few jobs as a research assistant. (Think creative services.) The money was good and some of the assignments proved interesting. I helped Nick expose a scam artist who sold phony home-security systems, and we nailed a crooked deputy sheriff who was scamming the county. Not exactly Sherlock Holmes stuff, but it beat serving burgers and fries. Between my freelancing and the jobs Nick threw my way, I was getting by.

"Are you calling from Boston?" I said.

"No, I'm in Monterey at the Thomas Larkin Hotel on Cannery Row. Is your office near here?"

That was a question I tend to hedge on. My office is basically the corner of the living room where my computer sits. The cottage I've been renting for the last five years is on Miles Avenue in Pacific Grove. It's a quiet woodsy area that abuts Del Monte Forest, home to Pebble Beach and a bundle of upscale golf courses.

"It's not far," I said. "Unfortunately, it's being refurbished. But I could meet you at your hotel."

"That would work."

"I could be there by eleven."

"Fine," she said, and hung up.

Fine with me, too. First I'd need to call Nick Allred and get some background on Nadine Stoughton. Before I could do that, the phone rang again.

I picked up, and this time said in a businesslike tone, "Preston Kane here, how may I help you?"

It was Nadine Stoughton again. "My suite number is 114," she said, "There's no need to check at the desk; you can come directly here."

She hung up as abruptly as before.

I waited a moment for another terse bulletin from Ms. Stoughton. None came, and I punched in Nick's number. I got his answering machine, thanked him for the referral, and said I'd get in touch later.

I'd be making a cold reading of my potential client, but since Nick had given her my name, I figured she was legit. And judging from my brief conversation with her, she was a woman of few words. A no-nonsense Bostonian.

I'd soon know if I was going to make a few bucks.

⁓⁓

Once while discussing with a friend our separate and tedious dealings with the California Department of Motor Vehicles, I mentioned that I'd never failed a driving test. "That's odd," she said, "considering what a lousy driver you are."

"Me?" I said. "What makes you say that?"

"Don't be defensive," she said. "It doesn't mean you're not a good person. But you're herky-jerky. You drive in fits and starts; step on the gas, let up on the gas. You drive too slow in the passing lane. You weave from one lane to another. You turn without signaling. You inspire other drivers to honk at you—and they're not just saying hello." She shook her head. "Should I go on?"

"Not really," I said. Her line of thinking could only lead to a discussion of such shortcomings as, say, inadequate parallel-parking skills.

I thought of her that morning after I succeeded—in my third attempt—to squeeze into a metered parking space a few doors down from the Thomas Larkin Hotel. Not an unusual memory trigger.

Many things made me think of her.

In the mid-1940s, John Steinbeck wrote: "Cannery Row in Monterey in California is a poem, a stink, a grating noise, a quality of light, a tone, a habit, a nostalgia, a dream."

The stink back in Steinbeck's day came from the sardines that kept the canneries busy. It was the smell of money, an intoxicating and welcome aroma. That scent is still heavy on the Row, but now it comes from another kind of fish—the tourists who flock to the mile-long waterfront street.

The Row follows the shoreline of Monterey Bay. At one end is the multi-million-dollar Monterey Bay Aquarium; near the other end is the elegant Monterey Plaza Hotel and Spa. In between, merchants peddle T-shirts, postcards, knick-knacks, and nachos.

If the Row is a tourist trap, at least it's clean. It also has some good restaurants. But the character of the place that Steinbeck had sung about in his hymn to the common man is gone. And so are the sardines.

The Thomas Larkin Hotel sits two blocks above Cannery Row, a short walk from the Aquarium and the Plaza Hotel. It's smaller and more intimate than the Plaza, but equally elegant. Crystal chandeliers hang from the ceilings. The parquet floors and dark wood paneling on the walls speak of an earlier day—a time when well-dressed gents could fill a room with billows of smoke from their expensive cigars and not feel a twinge of guilt.

About a year ago, I'd been a guest at the Larkin myself. Not *by* myself, though. I'd shared a suite with Cameron Dumont, the woman who'd criticized my driving skills. It was a honeymoon suite, although our visit marked an ending, not a beginning. Cam and I had been hanging out together for about two years. She was an executive at a local television station then, and she was attractive, intelligent, and witty—acerbically so. She was all-around good company. We were both in our mid-thirties and both divorced. Over time we co-evolved from good friends to cautious lovers, each leery of commitment. And before either of us knew where our relationship was going, it was over. There was friction between her and the general manager at her station. She happened to be in the right; he happened to be the owner's son. After a week of negotiations about her severance pay, she submitted her resignation. Our stay at the Larkin was something of a farewell party. A week later I drove her to San Francisco International Airport and watched her board a flight to Chicago, where she'd been hired as a TV news producer.

When I entered the Larkin, a dozen or so guests were gathered next to the front desk. Their luggage was clustered in the center of the lobby. A middle-aged man in new Nike running shoes and a fresh-off-the-rack tracksuit stood guard over it.

He noticed me and broke into a smile. "Excuse me," he said, "can I ask you a question?"

Did I look like a tour guide? Maybe. I was wearing my interview outfit: blue blazer, tan slacks, white shirt, maroon tie, black penny loafers.

"You already have," I said.

"Have what?"

"Never mind," I said. "What's up?"

He stuck a giveaway map of the Monterey Peninsula in my direction. "Can you tell me how to get to the Hog's Breath Inn?"

"Sure."

It's a frequently asked question on the Monterey Peninsula. One of the Hog's Breath's owners is Clint Eastwood. I took out my ballpoint pen and marked an X on the map. "It's on the west side of San Carlos, between Fifth and Sixth. They don't use street numbers in Carmel."

"Do you think—"

"Absolutely," I said. I looked at my watch. "In the middle of brunch now. Get there by noon and you'll catch him."

"Thanks," he said. With a smile on his face and his treasure map in hand, he returned to his luggage-guarding duties.

The desk clerk's tan looked store bought, and despite his gray hair, I pegged him to be about thirty. He was absorbed in a magazine, his lips pursed, his head tipped forward. I didn't disturb him.

Carpeted corridors branched off either side of the lobby. Above the portal to the corridor on the right was a burnished brass plate with black numbering enameled on it: 100—124. I passed under it and followed the corridor until I came to suite 114. The door was ajar. From inside came the sounds of classical music. I knocked hard, but there was no answer. I knocked harder. Still no answer.

I stepped inside and closed the door behind me. It looked much like the suite Cam and I had shared. I could hear the shower running. Although discretion isn't my strong suit, I opted for it this time. I headed for the glass doors, slid them open, and stepped out onto the balcony, keeping my back to the suite.

It was one of those terrific fog-free days that can bless the Monterey Peninsula in summer. A day when the usually cool breezes off the bay feel like warm velvet against your skin. To the right, the pale yellow grass on the slopes of the Gabilan Mountains glistened. Across the bay, to the left, the dark blue of the Santa Cruz Mountains stood out against the light blue of the sky.

Once on a similar day, a hardcore ex-New Yorker friend described the Monterey Peninsula to me as "a beautifully decorated wedding cake."

Before I could tell him he was mellowing, he added, "And one slice is enough."

⁓

A voice said, "Mr. Kane?" and I turned.

CHAPTER 2

I gasped. I'd have been crazy not to.

She was barefoot and wearing a white terrycloth bathrobe. A damp curl of red hair protruded from the white towel wrapped turban fashion about her head.

When the Renaissance painter Botticelli looked upon a woman like that, he pictured her as Venus emerging from the sea on a scallop shell. He, of course, was thinking like an artist. I guessed this wet woman had just stepped from the shower.

She stopped about three steps into the room and brought her hand to her mouth. "You *are* Preston Kane, I hope."

I found the gesture contrived, but charming. It allowed her robe to gape open several inches.

"I am," I said.

"Of course." She crossed the room and extended her hand. "I'm Nadine Stoughton. God, you got here so quickly."

I'd recognized the New England accent when she'd phoned me. It wasn't the nasal Cape Cod accent I'd grown up with, nor the flat, Irish-American inflection that Jack Kennedy had spoken. It was more finishing-school English—the sound one made in Boston when one had *cullchuh*.

"Nice to meet you," I said. She held the handshake for a moment and raised the other hand to tuck the wandering curl under the edge of the towel. The movement widened the interesting gap in her bathrobe. The flash of white flesh was ever-so-lightly decorated with freckles. I tried to look businesslike.

"If you can wait just a sec …" she said. She turned and popped into the bedroom. A moment later she popped back out, toting a book with a bright blue leatherette cover. It was one of those photo albums with the self-adhesive acetate pages.

She handed it to me, said, "Be right with you," and went back to the bedroom.

I sat down on the couch and opened the album. I didn't get far. I was still on the second page when she reappeared. She'd taken off the towel, and her damp hair was pulled straight back and held by a clip. A few stray ringlets framed her face. Her robe was now snugged tight, which was just as well. With that distraction out of the way, I could turn my attention to her eyes. Emerald green. Stunning.

She sat down next to me. "You don't have to bore yourself with the whole thing. Let me walk you through the good parts."

I inhaled and caught the scent of something exotic and, no doubt, expensive.

The phone in the bedroom rang, and she stood up. "Wouldn't you know? Excuse me, please." She headed for the bedroom again.

I sat there with the album in my lap and waited for her to reappear. After half a minute or so, I decided it wouldn't hurt to glance through the album without her. I could still let her walk me through the good parts.

The first section of the album contained clippings from a number of prominent newspapers and magazines, some obscure weeklies, and a couple of jewelry-trade journals. There was a clip from a year-old *Fortune* magazine. One from *People* magazine was only a month old.

Nadine Stoughton, it turned out, was one of the Stoughton Jewelry Stoughtons. I made an oohing sound. The Stoughtons were worth an ooh. At one time their chain of jewelry stores spread throughout New England, with the mother store a dominant presence on Boston's Boylston Street. They'd also had stores in New York and Beverly Hills. Once had, but no more. About a year ago, after the death of her father—Endicott Stoughton, Jr.—Nadine sold off the stores. A big chunk of the estate went to charities. But according to *Fortune,* the bulk of it—some twenty-eight million dollars—went to her.

A caption under a *People* photo described her father as "a leading American sportsman." He stood next to a flower-wreathed horse. He held a glass of champagne in one hand and a magnum of it in the other. His nose belonged in a potato patch—or in the middle of the actor Karl Malden's face. He looked sloshed.

Lucky Nadine. She must have had a beautiful mother. On the surface, she and her father had little in common except, perhaps, an affinity for the jewelry trade. Although there were no more Stoughton Jewelry outlets, the Stoughton Jewelry Salon she oversaw was, according to *People,* "a moveable feast of exquisite jewelry."

I didn't know what that meant. I read further: "It's a high-end road show of elegant gems. Nadine flies across the country—and to foreign countries and principalities as well—to service her exclusive clientele.

"Her events are invitation-only affairs. The most recent was 'The Night of the Windsor Star,' presented at the Helmsley Towers in New York City. It was a tribute to a diamond brooch valued at $3.5 million.

"Following a lavish dinner party—music courtesy of the Julliard String Quartet—the Windsor Star was displayed. To the disappointment of some guests, it was not for sale. An unnamed Middle Eastern sheik had purchased it earlier that day—for an unnamed price. Many guests eased their grief by scoring lesser baubles."

And so on.

The second half of the album was filled with glossy photographs of jewelry.

Before I got into it, Nadine called from the bedroom. "Mr. Kane, room service should be coming by with brunch. Would you sign for it, please? I've got to make a phone call."

"Okay," I said, hiding my disappointment at the delay. I was eager to go over the good parts with her.

I returned to the photo section and leafed through it. It was impressive. Each 8"x10" photograph presented a single piece of jewelry. The lighting was subtle, tasteful. Beneath each photograph, in elegant cursive, was a description of the piece.

When a knock sounded, I set the album on the coffee table and went to the door.

A young waiter with a serving cart stood in the hallway. I nodded to him, and he rolled the cart into the room. He pointed toward the covered dish that sat in the center of a silver serving tray.

"What is it?" I said.

He didn't speak, but pointed again and stepped away from the cart. His nametag said "James."

Did he understand English? Was he deaf? Was he a mute?

"Okay, James," I said. "No need for idle chatter." I stepped between him and the cart and reached for the handle of the covered dish.

He giggled, and I wondered how funny the brunch special could be.

I never found out. When I lifted the cover, the bastard cold-cocked me.

***

For the last five years I've known where I was when I woke up. This time it took me a while to get my bearings.

I finally got them. I was flat on my back, staring up at the underside of a box-spring mattress. I eased my way out from under the bed, stood up, and looked around. The drapes in the bedroom were open. I could see beams of sunlight glinting off the whitecaps in Monterey Bay. With each glint a crystal shard pierced my brain. I moved my hand to the focus of the pain, a lump that would have felt at home overlooking the Strait of Gibraltar.

It began to come back to me.

"Nadine?" I whispered. I wasn't being discreet. I feared doing to my head what Ella Fitzgerald's high notes did to stemware.

There was no answer.

I made my way gingerly into the sitting room. Deserted. I went back to the bedroom and opened the door to the walk-in closet. Bare hangers, empty shelves. A towel and a terrycloth bathrobe were bunched up on the bathroom floor. The shower stall was damp. There were no other signs anyone had been there.

I touched the lump on my head again, and again regretted it.

I wandered back to the sitting room and looked around. Everything seemed in place, but the album was missing. Had there been an album? Had there been a redhead?

I let myself out and closed the door behind me. Damn! As soon as I heard the lock click I realized I should have wiped down the places I'd touched. If somebody had snatched Nadine Stoughton, I didn't want to be a suspect. I had a few friends in local law enforcement, but a few enemies too. One in particular—Raymond Scriven—had a real grudge against me. He was the deputy sheriff Nick Allred and I had blown the whistle on a year-and-a-half ago.

Scriven's scam was simple—and simple-minded. He'd made an arrangement with a local contractor to use county equipment for grading a private building site. He let him into the county yard on a Friday night and the guy borrowed a county backhoe and some other equipment he needed to grade the site. He was supposed to return it all by Sunday night.

Saturday night, Nick heard about the operation through a tipster who wanted to be anonymous. Whether the tipster was public-spirited or just didn't like Scriven, I don't know. But I know Nick is public-spirited. He took the job on for free, paying me out of his own pocket. He didn't know Scriven or the developer, but he didn't like the idea of anybody ripping off taxpayers and abusing public office.

Sunday morning I took photos of the contractor using the backhoe, and Nick contacted the sheriff's office. We nailed both the contractor and Scriven, though not as hard as Nick wanted. The contractor was part of that sometimes blatant, sometimes shadowy, good-old-boy network that you often find in rural areas. He pulled weight and got off with a fine and a bill for the use of the equipment.

Scriven walked too, pretty much. They suspended him for two weeks without pay—a slap on the wrist. They figured if they let the contractor go, they'd have to let him go, too. I heard through the grapevine that most of the cops in the area thought Scriven should have been bounced. A few others supported him. They said Nick and I had stuck our noses into business that could have been better handled within the department.

Yeah, right.

I'd run across Scriven a few times since then, and he'd never said a word to me. He didn't need to; his glare did the job. I was sure nothing would please him more than a chance to put the screws to Nick and me.

But now I had other concerns than Scriven. Both my life and my livelihood had been threatened, and I was more angry than worried. I headed for the front desk. Maybe the clerk could tell me how to find Nadine Stoughton. She'd upped the weirdness level in my life a notch. She owed me some answers.

First question: What had she really wanted when she phoned me that morning?

CHAPTER 3

Years ago I read a story about an English tourist who disappeared on a trip to Naples. She vanished from her hotel, leaving no evidence that she'd ever been there. The woman's daughter tried to find out what happened to her mother, but to no avail. The manager and staff of the hotel claimed the mother had never checked in. In collusion with the police, they treated the daughter like a mental case. Finally the young woman gave up and went back to England.

The explanation was simple—and logical—if you know anything about the hospitality industry and the bubonic plague. Dying of the latter is what prompted her disappearance. The Neapolitan Chamber of Commerce—or its equivalent—hushed up the matter. Why get the tourist trade antsy? They cremated her body and deep-sixed the ashes in the Gulf of Naples.

In that story of a vanished lady, there was no sap-wielding waiter. My urban myth was of a different order.

When I got to the desk, the clerk was still occupied with his magazine. It was *GQ*, the current issue. I got a whiff of his cologne. Heady. I made a bet with myself that it was one of *GQ*'s top three picks. I stood there a moment. When it became apparent he wasn't going to acknowledge my presence, I said, "Do you have a bubonic plague problem here?"

He looked up. "What?"

"Could you tell me when Nadine Stoughton checked out?"

"She hasn't," he said, and slid back into his *GQ*.

I cleared my throat. "I just left suite 114. It was empty."

He looked up. "It still is. And has been since yesterday. Ms. Stoughton is in suite 110."

"That can't be."

"It can, trust me. I just finished talking with her."

"What?"

He looked at me as though I were a dim-witted child. "I … just … finished … talking … with … her." He gave me a weary smile. "I assume you're Mr. Kane?"

"Yeah."

"Well, Mr. Kane, she told me to tell you that if you weren't in her suite by 11:15, there'd be no sense in your being there at all." He checked his watch. "That gives you about fifty-five seconds."

"Thanks," I said. "You're a prince." I turned and crossed the lobby.

Thirty seconds later I stood in front of suite 110. I knocked hard.

The door opened and the woman in the doorway said—in a voice now familiar to me—"You're late, Mr. Kane. Please come in."

I hesitated in the doorway, trying to match the voice to the face. "I'm sorry, Ms. Stoughton," I said. "I ran into some trouble."

That didn't seem to interest her. "You may call me Nadine," she said. "I'm already behind schedule. Let's get started."

We moved to the sitting-room couch, and I checked out the suite. It was the image of the one I'd been in earlier, except for the framed print on the wall, a reproduction of a Monet garden. The print in 114 had been a Cezanne, a still life of a wine bottle and apples. And the woman in 114 who'd impersonated Nadine earlier had done a terrific job with the voice. But she'd blown it with the looks.

This real Nadine Stoughton had inherited her father's potato nose. She was of full figure and gray haired—a far cry from Venus on the half-shell.

Nadine looked at my business card and frowned. "You're not a full-time investigator?"

"Uh, no," I said. "Not as such."

I'd picked up that expression years ago in the Army. Captain Ferris, a personnel officer at Fort Benning, Georgia, used it frequently. If you asked if he had any manila envelopes, he'd say, "Not as such."

Was it raining? "Not as such."

Did he like raw walrus meat? "Not as such."

Maybe he intended to come off as a master of specifics. Or maybe he used it for the same reason Army sergeants said "behoove"—because they liked the sound of it. I used it as a diversionary tactic. Nadine wasn't diverted. "That's not the end of the world," she said. "In fact, your not being a full-time detective could be an advantage."

If my not being a detective was a good reason for hiring me as a detective, I wasn't going to argue. I indicated that with a brisk nod.

Dumb. A jolt of pain radiated from the back of my skull and shot angry dispatches to the base of my neck and the crown of my head.

Nadine ignored my grimace. She tapped my business card with one finger and cocked her head back, as though seeking inspiration in the pattern of ceiling tiles. "Perhaps it would put him off his guard if he thought you were simply doing some writing for me— PR work, say."

"Who's he?"

She stood up. "Just a moment," she said, and headed off to the bedroom.

Although I'd just seen *Back to the Future* at the Dream Theater in New Monterey, I try my best to make distinctions between movies and real life. Still, my feelings of uneasiness were edging into the realm of dread. If she came out in a terrycloth bathrobe, I'd do a vanishing act.

I didn't need to. When she returned, she was still wearing a navy blue suit over a pale yellow blouse. But the album she held in her hands looked familiar.

"As you may know," she said, "I'm in the jewelry business."

I nodded.

She opened to the photo of the Windsor Star and handed the album to me. "Take a look at this."

A knock on the door sounded, and she said, "Come in." She turned to me. "It must be room service."

The door swung open and a woman came in bearing a silver tray with rolls and coffee. I felt a jolt of adrenaline as I flashed back to the waiter who'd bopped me earlier.

My god! What kind of paranoid thinking was I getting into?

I ran a quick reality check. The current perceived threat in the apron weighed about eighty pounds and was probably thirty years my senior. Did I blush? I felt I should. Still, I eyed her warily until she took the signed tab from Nadine and left.

"Do you take anything in your coffee?" Nadine said.

"No, thanks, black is fine."

She poured for both of us and set the pot down. She took a sip from her cup and frowned. She added a heaping spoonful of sugar and said, "Two clients from this area are seeking the Windsor Star."

"I thought an Arabian sheik owned it."

"He did—on paper. Events in the Mideast prevented him from coming up with the cash. I own it again."

"And who wants to buy it?"

"Do you know who Peter Cobb and Jerry Racker are?"

Who didn't? The two Silicon Valley whiz kids had founded Cobra Tech, a computer software company that had revolutionized a revolutionary industry. Along the way they'd made jillions.

"I know of them," I said. "But as I understand it, they aren't on speaking terms." Last year, their split had been a high-tech shocker for the media. After an eight-year partnership and friendship, Racker had forced Cobb off the board of Cobra and bought him out. It had been ugly. Now Cobb had his own company—Mongoose Systems. The name suggested his plans for his former partner.

Nadine smiled. "They loathe each other. And they each want the Windsor Star. That puts me in an enviable position."

"It goes to the highest bidder."

"Exactly. Two days from now, there'll be a telephone auction."

"You want me to check out Cobb and Racker?"

"No. First I want you to give me some background information on Foster Bingham. He's the lawyer who will conduct the auction. When you've done that, I think a call to the other two might be in order."

Foster "Binx" Bingham. I'd never met him, but I'd seen his photo often enough in the *Monterey Eagle*, the local daily I used to work for. He was a real estate lawyer and on the board of half a dozen local nonprofit organizations. A solid citizen from an old Monterey family.

"You think he's—"

"I don't think anything at the moment," Nadine said. "Mr. Bingham was recommended by my law firm in Boston. Supposedly he's above reproach, but there's a good deal of money involved in this situation, and I just want to make sure Mr. Bingham isn't dining at two tables—or, in this case, three."

"You want to know if he might hold down the price in exchange for a kickback."

"I want to make sure he's playing straight."

"Any suggestions?"

"Yes. I want you to find out if he's been in touch with either Mr. Cobb or Mr. Racker. He's been told not to contact them. If he has been in touch—for whatever reason—I don't want him working for me."

"How will he set up the auction then?"

"My people in Boston have arranged it. Mr. Bingham's role is to act as auctioneer and to close the deal. I've told neither Mr. Cobb nor Mr. Racker that I hired Mr. Bingham. If there's been any such contact, Mr. Bingham would have had to initiate it."

I nodded.

"After you speak with Mr. Bingham, you could contact Mr. Cobb and Mr. Racker and try to determine if he's approached them."

She took a card from her purse and handed it to me. "Here are numbers for their private lines, and the codes for getting through to them. "You can probably reach Mr. Cobb during the day. Mr. Racker's a night owl—an old-fashioned programmer. You can try him anytime between ten at night and ten in the morning."

"How should I contact Mr. Bingham without his getting suspicious?"

"I'll call him and tell him I'm sending a publicist to see him to get background on the sale. That's true, by the way. I will want something written up on the sale—press releases and so on. Mr. Allred said you could handle that."

She took my card from the table and looked at it again. "I assume you'd be interested in that."

"Certainly. My rates are different for—"

"You don't have to go into the details. Just give me a final invoice."

That was heartening, but no more tangible than a future check in the mail.

"Certainly," I said. "But I'll need an advance."

"Fine," she said. She pulled a checkbook from her purse. "Will five hundred dollars be sufficient?"

"Absolutely," I said—and I meant it. I'd been prepared to ask for two hundred. I felt a surge of warmth at the thought of what bliss a simple paper instrument from a financial institution brings.

She handed me the check and knitted her brow. She pointed to the bump on my head. "You mentioned you'd run into some trouble."

I hesitated. The events were so outlandish, I worried she'd think I was a wack job if I told her what actually happened. But she'd played straight with me, and I decided to give it a shot.

"This may be a bit hard to swallow," I said, and I laid it all out for her.

—⁓—

When I finished, she said, "That story is only slightly harder to swallow than a porcupine—but for some reason I believe you. Did you notify the police?"

"No."

"Do you intend to?"

"I don't see much point in it," I said. Which was true. There were no witnesses to my being slugged, so it'd be hard to prove assault. What else could I complain about? I'd been titillated and duped; that was about it. I didn't think T&D cases were a high priority for our local crime busters.

She nodded. "I think you're right. And from my point of view, I'd rather not have the negative publicity. Still, if you think—"

"I'd rather not have it either," I said.

"Good. That's a peculiar story you told me, Preston—may I call you that?"

I nodded.

"*Very* peculiar," she said, "but we're dealing with very peculiar people."

"Mr. Cobb and Mr. Racker?"

"Yes." She crossed her arms and leaned toward me. "Among the very rich—especially the *nouveau* very rich—life gets magnified. They'll do things you and I might think irrational."

I felt flattered that she'd included me in the same bag as herself and her twenty-eight million dollars. "But why such a crazy set-up?" I said.

"Perhaps one of them sought information that could give him an advantage. That's the coin they deal in."

"But a farfetched scheme—"

"Remember," she said, "they got their start inventing clever computer games."

"True."

"On the other hand, maybe it was someone else entirely, some-one with different motives. Maybe even someone who thought you might have the Windsor Star in your possession."

"Bingham?"

She shook her head. "No. He knows the Star is in the vault of my bank in Boston—where it will remain until the sale is completed."

"Any idea who else it could be?"

She shook her head. "Not the slightest."

I stood up. "Unless you have something else for me, I'll get in touch with Bingham."

"Good," she said, "I'll call him now and set up an appointment." She took a leather address book from her purse. "Before I call Mr. Bingham, is there anything else you need to know?"

I picked up the photo album. "Are there any more of these?"

"Yes, we sent out more than a hundred of them to selected clients. You may have that one. It might be helpful for your PR work."

"Thank you," I said. "Oh—and a point of curiosity—how did you happen to contact Mr. Allred?"

"The Yellow Pages," she said. "His was the first listing. We talk-ed briefly, and he seemed like a reasonable, intelligent, and honest man."

Nick was all that.

And Nadine Stoughton was a true no-nonsense Bostonian.

I liked her.

CHAPTER 4

The Monterey Public Library sits catty-corner from City Hall and directly across the street from the city's fire department and police station. I walked in the front entrance and went directly to the reference desk. I didn't have much time to do my homework. In twenty minutes I'd be meeting Foster Bingham at the Commonwealth Club on Tyler Street, a few blocks from the library.

My friend Bill Kittering was manning the desk, looking natty and ghastly in a button-down black shirt and white tie. Bill's a demon marathon runner, and he makes your average gaunt guy look chubby. I gave him my library card and told him I wanted to use the California Room, the reference room on the second floor that contains historical material, most of it about the Monterey area.

Bill paper-clipped my card to the register and logged me in. "You can go right up," he said.

"It's not locked?"

"Shouldn't be." He glanced at the register. "Someone signed in an hour ago, and she hasn't checked out. If it *is* locked, come down and get me and I'll unlock it for you."

"You want me to climb the stairs *twice?*"

Bill gave me a death's head grin. "The exercise will do you good."

"That's your theory."

I headed for the stairs.

———

The California Room has an old-timey library ambience that appeals to me. Its shelves house ancient books with cracked leather bindings, yellowed pages, and musty auras that identify the room as an authentic archive of the past. It's always about ten degrees cooler there than in the rest of the library. That's not usually a plus, but it's refreshing during the rare heat spells, like the one we were now going through. It's dusty, of course. I sneezed as soon as I stepped through the doorway. An elderly woman sat at the table nearest the door, her head resting on the open book in front of her. She bolted upright and smiled at me.

She was a tweedy sort. I couldn't see her shoes, but it was likely they were sensible and sturdy. A pheasant feather adorned her green felt hat. Its rakish angle made her look like Robin Hood's kindly grandmother.

"Excuse me," I said, and returned her smile.

She nodded and dropped her head back on the book.

I went to the file cabinets that held local biography. I opened the "B" drawer and riffled through it. The section on Binghams took up about a quarter of the drawer. The folders on Cyrus Bingham were packed with documents, many in the crumbly stage. There were smaller folders on Maxwell Bingham, Stanton Bingham, and Foster Bingham—all descendants of Cyrus. I started with him.

The first document was a twelve-page monograph written for the WPA Writers' Project in 1941. I was familiar with Monterey County history, but the monograph filled in some gaps.

———

That old Yankee Ralph Waldo Emerson wrote: "If a man is going to California, he announces it with some hesitation, because it is a confession that he has failed at home."

That wasn't the case with Cyrus Bingham. He'd done just fine at home. He'd made a fortune during the Civil War by importing cotton cloth from Egypt. He sold it to New England clothing manufacturers, who made military uniforms from it. He then stepped back into the picture and brokered the uniforms to the Union Army.

When the war was over, Cyrus spent a few years in other ventures back East, none so lucrative as his wartime activities had been. Eventually he decided he'd use the know-how he'd acquired in the cotton importing business to import silk from China. He set out for San Francisco, planning to use that city as his base of operations. An opportunity in Monterey convinced him to change his plans.

He teamed up with David Jacks, a transplanted Scotsman who'd mastered the not-so-gentle art of land-grabbing. Over the years, both Jacks and Bingham were subjected to hangings-in-effigy and other well-intentioned death threats from embittered Montereyans who felt they'd been ripped off by the two. They were both wily enough to avoid the real thing.

Bingham speculated in land, raised some cattle, and waxed rich—although not so rich as Jacks. Along the way he married the daughter of a Presbyterian minister and sired one son, Maxwell. Cyrus Bingham died in 1918, at the age of seventy-seven, a victim of the influenza pandemic that was sweeping the world.

Both the names of Jacks and Bingham live on in the Monterey area. Jacks Peak Park now occupies more than 500 acres on the mountain ridge that divides Carmel Valley from Monterey. In downtown Monterey there's the Bingham Foundation, Bingham Court, and the Foster Bingham Law Firm.

I didn't know how much of the family holdings were left, but I knew Foster Bingham lived at *El Rancho de los Lobos*—The Ranch of the Wolves—built by grandfather Cyrus in the 1890s. The *lobos*, by the way, weren't the four-legged type. The place was named for the *lobos del mar*—wolves of the sea—or sea lions. Their barking can still be heard throughout the Monterey Peninsula when the wind is right. Or wrong. It depends on how you feel about marine mammal chatter.

I checked my watch and put the monograph back in the file. I'd get to Foster Bingham's folder later. In ten minutes I'd be having lunch with him.

I closed the file cabinet drawer and tiptoed out of the room. Downstairs, I signed out at the reference desk and left through the rear door. I crossed the library's back parking lot and took the dirt path that runs between the side wall of the old Stokes Adobe and Hartnell Creek. A sullen young man sat with his back against the wall, his legs extending into the path. He was frantically rearranging the colors on a Rubik's Cube, which I assumed was why he'd cut the fingertips of his black leather gloves. His dyed black hair matched his Gothic clothing. Each nostril held a small golden ring. A larger one hung from the septum.

When I stepped over his outstretched legs, he tipped his head to the side and graced me with a sneer. The sun glinted off the rings. A dazzling effect. Once flu season started, I thought, it might be less so.

"Get a flu shot," I said, bonding with the hope for the future. I continued on toward the Commonwealth Club to bond with the hopes of the past.

CHAPTER 5

At 12:55 I climbed the brick front steps of the Commonwealth Club and knocked on the door. Perfect timing. More than prompt, less than eager.

The club is housed in a two-story adobe that dates back to the early1840s—after the Mexicans had booted out the Spanish colonizers, but before the gringos gave the Mexicans the boot. From the street, you can't tell it's a private club. A small wooden sign on the front door indicates it's open to the public. The building, that is. The club leases the historical landmark from the city. In return, the members pay for its upkeep and grant visiting privileges to tourists and other riffraff. Three hours on Saturday morning. For the rest of the week, it's inhabited mostly by well-to-do white men.

Despite the name, it's not connected with the Commonwealth Club in San Francisco. The Monterey club was founded in 1911 by three Stanford alumni, emigrants from the Commonwealth of Virginia who wanted to honor their roots. They attached cabalistic significance to the number ninety-six—1896 being the year the three graduated from Stanford—and that's what the club's membership is limited to. A member has to die before a new one's admitted. Needless to say, there's a long waiting list of men whose goals include growing older and getting richer.

Local wags refer to the organization as the Uncommonly Wealthy Club.

I stepped through the doorway, and an Asian man in a server jacket approached me. He looked to be about seventy-five. "Good afternoon, sir," he said. "May I help you?"

"I'm Preston Kane," I said. "I have a lunch appointment with Foster Bingham."

He nodded and flashed some gold teeth at me. "Wait, please." He tottered off down the hallway, and I was left to admire the decor. It was admirable.

The building was one of the classic Monterey Colonials scattered throughout the city. If its interior suggested Old New England more than Old Monterey, that wasn't surprising. Boston merchant Thomas Oliver Larkin—the guy they named the Thomas Larkin Hotel after—had set the style after arriving in Monterey in the early 1830s. It wouldn't be the last change he or his ilk would make in the Golden Land of Califia.

A mid-nineteenth century painting of Monterey Custom House official Joaquin Gutierrez hung by the entrance. The somber look on his face suggested he'd figured out what Larkin and the other Yankee traders had in mind for his town.

"Mr. Kane?" a voice said.

I turned and recognized Foster Bingham from photographs I'd seen. About forty, he stood a little over six feet tall. His face was tanned, which set off his light blue eyes. He had the look of a man who played enough golf and tennis to stay in shape without having to work out at a gym.

He extended his hand. "I'm Foster Bingham," he said, and flashed one of those open smiles that made you want to smile back.

That's what I did. "Preston Kane," I said. "Nice to meet you."

We shook hands and I checked out his tie, an expensive dark blue silk number with a pattern of little red golf clubs. They could as well have been dollar signs.

"Care for something at the bar?" He gestured toward the room he'd just come from.

"No thanks. But I'll join you if you'd like something."

"That's all right," he said. "My stomach's growling, anyway."

He led me into another hallway.

The club members took their lunch buffet-style. A modified steam table was set up on one side of the hallway, a salad bar on the other.

A man about Bingham's height was coming our way, balancing a salad dish, dinner plate, and cup of soup. Bingham gave him a wink. "Hey, Big Bull."

The man returned the wink. "Hey, Big Bear." He squeezed by us and gave *me* a wink. I nodded, smiled. I didn't feel quite as comfortable with the wink business as these Commonwealthers did.

When the man was out of hearing range, Bingham said, "Charlie Walsh, stockbroker—an extremely important man in town." The hint of a smile suggested he was presenting Walsh's opinion, not his own. I'd seen Walsh's picture in the paper as often as Bingham's. Same reasons. Heading this committee, attending that social function, and so on.

I turned my attention to the food. It looked good. Poached salmon filets and some kind of sautéed-chicken dish. When I was a lad, my father told me there was no such thing as a free lunch. He added, "But if you find something like it, don't order the blue-plate special."

I dropped a sizable hunk of salmon on my plate and hit the salad bar for some Salinas Valley lettuce and cold green beans. I passed on the clam chowder. It looked like it had been thickened with flour—intolerable to a Cape Cod chowder snob.

Another pan contained what looked like cream of wheat. I leaned closer. "Is that what I think it is?"

Bingham laughed. "Grits—a traditional dish here, but don't ask me why. Maybe it got started during the war. This place is rife with odd traditions."

"I ate grits at Fort Benning," I said. "They weren't bad." I scooped a smidgeon onto my plate, as much for sentimental reasons as anything else.

Bingham wrinkled his nose. "They tried to force them on me at Fort Rucker. They didn't succeed."

Bingham led the way through a large oak-paneled room and into an outdoor courtyard. It was enclosed by the main building on one side and by twelve-foot-high adobe brick walls on the other three. A dozen or so tables set with linen and silverware were scattered about the courtyard. Two long ones had eight settings. The rest were laid out for four people. Bingham beckoned me to one of those, where two men were already seated.

"Roger," Bingham said to a fiftyish man with a ruddy face. "I'd like you to meet a friend. Roger Newsome, Preston Kane."

"Roger's in the insurance game," Bingham said. He gestured toward me. "Preston's a writer. He's doing some public relations work for one of my clients."

"That must be grand," Newsome said. "I wish I had time to write."

I didn't wish I had time to sell insurance, so I just smiled.

The other man at the table could have passed for a chipper one-hundred-and-ten. He kept his head down and dug into his salmon. He ate as though it might be his last meal. He'd probably been suspecting that for some time.

When Bingham was through introducing Newsome and me, the old guy looked up and said in a quavering voice, "Binx."

Bingham gave the countersign—"Phippy"—and introduced us.

I'd seen Philip "Phippy" Southworth's name and face in the paper for years. A jolly old elf he appeared. But I hadn't comprehended how small he was until I took his hand in mine. I thought of a monkey's paw. I also thought of the Southworth Cruise Lines. His grandfather had been pals with "The Big Four"— railroad tycoons from California's 19th century robber-baron days.

Phippy.
Binx.

The kind of prep school nicknames rich people love. But with a nickname like Presto, I couldn't complain. Mine didn't come from prep school, though. It wasn't even derived from "Preston," as many of my acquaintances assumed. I sometimes told people I'd picked it up in my youth because magic was my hobby. It had in fact been my hobby for a while, but that's not where the name came from. Its origin is a high spot in my family saga.

When I was about four, I strolled into the living room during a cocktail party my parents were throwing. I'd just stepped from my bath and had a towel wrapped around me. When the guests turned to admire my cuteness, I dropped the towel and revealed an erection.

"Presto!" I announced.

And Presto I became.

Family nicknames can be embarrassing, but mine could have been worse. Consider the Mafia crime family turncoat Jimmy "The Weasel" Fratianno.

After the introduction, Southworth returned to his plate, offering us a bird's-eye view of the crown of his shapeless tennis hat. On the way into the courtyard I'd passed a hat rack that held a half-dozen goofy hats like that. They were loaners, for anyone who needed one. They served a useful purpose: protecting old palefaces from the sun. But beyond that, as hats often do, they served as caste marks. A few years back, Nick Allred brought that to my attention. He pointed to an old codger who was leaving a bank in downtown Pacific Grove. He wore a ludicrous mouse-gray slouch hat. The brim drooped to his shoulders. Weird headgear for sure, but there was no chance the guy would be taken for an oddball. His expensive shoes and cashmere sports coat told the world he was no eccentric. At least not a poor one. His outfit cost more than the compact gas hog I drove at the time.

"That hat," Nick said, "is a civilized way of saying to the world, 'I'm as rich as Rockefeller, and I can dress any way I want, no matter how silly I look.'"

Subtle. If I were that rich, I'd go for blatant. A jewel-encrusted crown might be nice.

———

There was a nearly empty carafe of white wine on the table. As soon as we were seated, another elderly Asian waiter appeared with a replacement.

"Thanks, Benny," Bingham said.

The waiter nodded and emptied the last drops of the first carafe into Newsome's glass. When he left, Newsome gave me a smile. "Benny's a real character," he said.

Southworth raised his head from his plate. "A good boy."

Bingham reached for the fresh carafe, and turned to me. "Care for a taste?"

"No thanks."

"Bit early in the day."

I said nothing. When you don't drink, people who do drink tend to think you're judging them. They're right. I judged that Bingham would have one glass of wine with lunch and not have another drink until dinner. That had never been my style, but more power to him.

Newsome, sitting to my left, was another story. There was a glass of wine next to Phippy Southworth's plate, but it was nearly full. I figured Newsome had put the major dent in the first carafe. I also figured that no matter how much wine Newsome drank during lunch, he'd leave his last glass half full. Back at work, time for a medicinal shot or two. After which, maybe a snooze on the couch in his private office while his secretary—"God, Angela's a gem. Don't know what I'd do without her."—diverted calls.

That was enough judging. I tucked into my salmon.

———

After Southworth and Newsome left, our waiter brought us

coffee and cleared the table—including Newsome's half-full glass of wine.

He filled my cup, and I stared at the liver spots and protruding veins on his hands. When he left, Bingham said, "Some boy, huh?"

"A real character," I said.

Bingham laughed. "Old Phippy's still locked into the nineteenth century. And poor Roger …." He let it ride and surveyed the courtyard. "You know," he said, "they might sound a bit … I don't know, racist, if you want to take it that way. But not by their lights. More than anything, they're out of touch. Hell, this club itself is a relic. I guess you could say most members just want a place to gather with people of their own backgrounds and interests."

He gave a wry smile. "Which, I suppose, is pretty much what the Black Panthers and the Ku Klux Klan want. Anyway, Nadine tells me you need some background information to put together a press release on the Windsor Star sale."

I nodded.

"That shouldn't be a problem. I can fill you in somewhat, and once the sale is completed, I can put you in touch with whichever boy genius gets the prize."

"Great."

Bingham took another sip of coffee and cocked his head to the side. "She said you've done some work for Nick Allred."

"That's right."

"Quite a fellow. In '77 I spent some hellish days with him during the Marble Cone fire in the Ventana Wilderness. He was heading a volunteer fire-fighting crew, and he worked our butts off. But he worked even harder himself. When we went home, he stayed on."

"Nick's a powerhouse, all right."

"He connect you with Nadine?"

I nodded.

"Bingham raised an eyebrow. "Your connection with Nick was in the area of investigations, right?"

"That, PR, and advertising work."

He slapped his palm on the table. "Oh hell, Preston," he said, "let's stop dancing around."

I shrugged.

"Nadine wants you to find out if I'm cutting deals with the computer kids."

They say a good lawyer never asks a question he doesn't already know the answer to. I knew Bingham was a good lawyer. "She's curious—and cautious," I said.

"Can't say I blame her. We're talking about substantial amounts of money. But the fact is, there's no hanky-panky involved."

"She didn't say there was."

"I shouldn't think so." He paused and looked down for a moment. "Preston," he said, "do you have any idea what the Windsor Star is worth?"

"Not really."

"It's worth precisely what any diamond's worth: whatever a buyer is willing to pay for it. In 1969 Richard Burton wanted to buy a nice present for his wife, Elizabeth Taylor. And he did. He paid one million dollars and some change for what became known as the Taylor-Burton Diamond. It was hefty, about seventy carats. Nine years later—after their *second* divorce—Liz sold it for an estimated five million dollars. A nice appreciation, wouldn't you say?"

"Nice indeed."

"In 1982," he said, "Nadine Stoughton paid two million dollars for the Windsor Star. It's smaller than the diamond Liz Taylor sold—about fifty-five carats—and the bidding on it will start at four million dollars. Each of the only two bidders is eager to buy it. They're both exceptionally wealthy, very competitive, and—as I'm sure you know—they hate each other. I'm set to earn a very decent percentage of the sale—guaranteed. I think you'll agree I'd be foolish to try to pull any hijinks."

"Very foolish."

Bingham smiled. "Look, I'm not irked that she's testing my integrity. I can stand up to it. I've got a good reputation in town, and I've earned it. Nadine isn't that familiar with me—we've only had one face-to-face meeting—and I can understand that she might feel a bit tentative about me. No harm there. The lawyer in Boston who steered her my way—Lew Stiles, an old Stanford chum of mine—told me a little about her. She's a tad on the eccentric side, but that can be an endearing quality. She's prudent, which is fine with me. From what Lew said, and from what I gathered in my meeting with her, she's astute, honest, and a decent person."

I nodded again. That was my take, too.

Bingham spread his hands, palms up. "So, with that out of the way, is there anything I can do for you?"

"As a matter of fact there is," I said. "I will actually be putting together publicity material for Nadine, and she said you might have some useful information I could use."

"I've got background material on Cobb and Racker. Probably nothing you couldn't find in the library. Also material on the Windsor Star itself that I got from Lew Stiles." He smiled. "And by the way, I do hold a bit of both Mongoose and Cobra stock, but Nadine is aware of that." He looked at his watch. "If you can stop by my office around four, I'll have something ready for you."

"Thanks. I'd appreciated it."

He looked out to the courtyard. About a dozen men were still seated at their tables, lingering over their coffee—goofy hats, Stanford ties, old money. With a casual hand gesture, Bingham encompassed it all. "They're the last vestiges of the golden age of capitalism," he said. "Regular dinosaurs. But quite frankly, I prefer them to the new generation of sharks."

I assumed that included Racker and Cobb.

CHAPTER 6

After I left the Commonwealth Club, I looked at the card Nadine Stoughton had given me with Cobb's and Racker's phone numbers.

Bingham knew Nadine had sent me to check up on him; therefore, if he were running a game with either Racker or Cobb, he'd have already alerted whichever one he was in cahoots with and told him I'd be calling.

By acknowledging that he knew Nadine was checking up on him, he'd given me an edge. But it would only be an edge if he were double-crossing Nadine. He was a smart cookie, and I didn't think he was in the habit of giving away much of anything. Therefore, he wasn't double-crossing Nadine.

That was my logic, anyway. Maybe it was faulty—I'm no stranger to faulty logic, as Cam Dumont might tell you. But beyond logic, my gut instinct told me that Bingham was on the level.

I'd still call Racker and Cobb, if only to satisfy Nadine, but I'd have to devise some other means of finding out if Bingham had been in touch with them. I hoped Bingham wasn't scamming Nadine, because I found him a likable guy. Not that he was your man-in-the-street by a long shot. He clearly fancied himself a cut above the common herd—even above his grit-eating pals at the Commonwealth Club. You wouldn't catch him eating poor-man's corn meal. And he seemed to be neither a pretentious fool nor a closet bigot.

Of course, I was comparing him to some extent with Newsome and Southworth—a dolt and a dotard—which had to tip the scales in his favor. Beyond that, though, he said he'd fought fires with Nick Allred. I'd ask Nick about him. If he okayed him, that would be a solid endorsement.

In the Army I'd met a few men like Bingham, guys from privileged backgrounds who—when they cared to—could fit in just fine with us rabble. Bingham had probably fit in just fine at Fort Rucker. I couldn't see him sloshing down 3.2 Falstaff beer at the EM club. Knocking back a few mint juleps on the veranda of the Officers' Club was more like it. But I bet he carried his own weight when he was out in the boondocks.

The thought of Fort Rucker took me back some twenty years to my own army days at Fort Benning, Georgia. Fort Rucker was in Alabama, about a two hour drive from Benning. I'd never been there, but a story about it had sent shivers up my spine. It still does.

As I heard it, a bunch of GIs from Rucker decided to cap a night on the town by taking a midnight skinny dip in a nearby swimming hole. The first guy to peel off his clothes dove into the water and came up about twenty feet from shore. He yelled, "Don't come in!" and sank from sight. He didn't surface again.

That sobered the others up. One of them hunted down a phone and called the military equivalent of 911. A rescue crew rushed to the scene, but they were too late to save the guy—or even find him.

The next day they dragged the pond and retrieved his body. It was covered with water-moccasin bites—more than fifty of them. He'd plunged into the middle of a reptilian mating orgy.

I only half-believed the story, but it was a nice creepy tale to repeat. And—my doubts about it notwithstanding—it kept me out of swimming holes for my entire tour of duty in the South.

Bingham had survived the South too, and he seemed to be doing just fine now. His part in the Windsor Star auction would add a tidy chunk to his holdings. I doubted he'd play games with Nadine Stoughton.

I wouldn't either. I'd pick up the stuff from Bingham's office and make the pro-forma calls she asked for. With the investigative work out of the way, I could get started on the promotional material. I wouldn't need to talk to Racker or Cobb again until after the auction. Maybe just to the winner.

I wondered which one it would be.

I soon found out.

On my way back to Pacific Grove, I had the radio tuned to an all-news station from San Francisco. Big news of the day: President Reagan announced we were sending the first schoolteacher into space as part of the NASA Teacher in Space Project.

The high school teacher, Christa McAuliffe, was from New Hampshire, and like Nadine Stoughton, a born Bostonian. I had no doubt she was a no-nonsense one too.

I'd have to give Nadine a call.

As I entered the Lighthouse Avenue tunnel, I lost reception and switched to the FM station KAZU. I caught the tail end of a local story. It was about Peter Cobb—the late Peter Cobb, whose body had washed up on a Pacific Grove beach.

I'd read in the local newspaper about some kid who'd found a floater a few days back. The body was beyond identification, a messy corpse with no face and mushy fingers. But—according to the radio report—the wetsuit the guy was wearing was an expensive French model. The cops checked out the local surf and dive shops and found one that carried that type. It was a big-ticket item, and they'd sold only one—to Peter Cobb. A check of dental records confirmed his identity.

So much for the bidding war.

So much for my five hundred dollar advance.

When I parked in front of my cottage, I saw the front door was ajar, and I sprinted up the walkway. I don't carry renter's insurance, because I own so little that anyone would want to steal—except for my computer. I stormed into the cottage and felt a burst of relief. My Kaypro II was still sitting in the corner. Without it I'd be screwed.

It's a self-contained portable computer that folds up into what looks like a metal suitcase. A hefty one. One of the techs at the dealership where I bought it claims it's great for sitting on when you can't find a seat in an airport waiting room. The package came with some games and all kinds of accounting stuff, but I only use it for word processing. It set me back about $1,500, but it's worth it.

I took a quick survey and nothing seemed disturbed. The answering machine was still on the bookshelf by the phone, and the blinking light indicated I had two calls. I hit the replay button and continued checking out the room.

As the machine squeaked and gibbered through a rewind, I wondered if I might be overreacting. The block I lived on was a quiet neighborhood, and I'd forgotten to lock the door in the past. In my hurry to get to the Larkin, maybe I hadn't even closed it.

The first call was from Nick Allred. He wanted to know how the meeting with Nadine went. He said he'd check back later.

The second call was from my Botticelli Venus. She wasn't doing her Nadine imitation, but I knew who she was. Her message was brief: "Mr. Kane, I'm sorry about what happened, but we have to talk. I'm coming to your house. If you pick this up on your remote, please hurry home. It's urgent."

My machine's mechanical voice told me the message had come in at 11:48. I tried to make sense of it and couldn't. She'd seen me a little after eleven that morning. Presumably she knew that the waiter had knocked me out. A half-hour or so after that, she'd called. She must have thought I'd be home by then, or that I'd be calling in for my messages. I had no idea what she wanted from me.

I stuck my head into the bedroom. Empty. Same with the kitchen. The bathroom door was closed. I reached for the knob, but a vision of the waiter came to me, and I stopped halfway.

I tiptoed into the kitchen and took a carving knife from the utensil rack above the sink. If the little bastard *was* in the bathroom, the eight-inch blade would give him food for thought. I held the knife in front of me, stood back from the bathroom door, and eased it open with my foot.

The shower curtain was closed. I was sure I'd left it open after my shower that morning.

I tried a variation of the old whistling-in-the-graveyard ploy. "I know you're in there," I said. "I'm armed, so come out slowly with your hands behind your head."

I waited. Till then I'd been unaware of the sounds from outside. Now I was conscious of traffic noise from a neighboring street, the drone of an airplane overhead, a scrub jay's nagging. But I couldn't hear anything or see any movement behind the shower curtain. I ducked into the kitchen and returned with a broom. I held the knife in my left hand and with the right extended the broom through the doorway. When it touched the shower-curtain ring nearest me, I thrust my arm forward. The rings rattled and the shower curtain gaped wide.

"Oh, Jesus!"

I dropped the broom and stared at my Botticelli Venus. Only she wasn't rising triumphantly from the sea. She lay on the floor of the shower stall, her head twisted upward, her eyes open and staring at the ceiling. They saw nothing.

I stepped into the bathroom and knelt by the shower stall. She wore a tan cotton blouse and a denim skirt. Back at the Larkin, I'd been struck by how beautiful her skin was. No longer. I'd heard that the Chinese consider white the color for death and mourning. Now I understood why.

I touched her face. I don't know what I expected, but I was shocked at how cold it felt. I took my hand away, and her head tipped forward. One of her earrings—a few turquoise beads strung on a short length of gold wire—rested against her neck. The flesh around it was discolored by ugly bruises.

As I tried to make sense of what I saw, a voice from the living room said, "Drop the knife, Kane, or I'll blow your head off!"

A man in a tan sheriff's uniform stood outside the bathroom door, his pistol pointing in my direction. It was Raymond Scriven, looking as repulsive as ever. You wouldn't be surprised to see him overseeing a Mississippi chain gang. He had piggy eyes and a nose that angled down from his forehead with no indentation to tell you exactly where it began. A policeman stood behind him.

I stood up and let the knife fall to the floor.

"Move back, asshole," Scriven said.

I did, and he edged forward, keeping the gun on me. He looked toward the shower and the expression on his face could have been one of shock—on anyone else it would have been—but as he turned to me, it seemed more like a leer.

I felt a surge of revulsion. It was like a nightmare coming true. I felt powerless against a creep who had the full power of the law behind him and a penchant for abusing it.

And what the hell was a deputy sheriff doing here, anyway? This was Pacific Grove PD territory

He looked me in the eye. "How sweet it is—"

He quick-stepped forward and swung the barrel of his pistol across my temple.

For the second time that day I hit the deck.

When I woke up, there were about a dozen blurry strangers in my cottage. I closed one eye and cut the number of uninvited guests in half. It made the house seem less crowded, but it didn't help my head any. The throbbing I'd felt back at the Larkin was kid stuff compared to this. I closed the other eye and turned my head slowly from side to side. When I opened them both again, the number of people held steady at six, and they weren't quite so blurry.

I don't know how I got there, but I was sitting in my fake leather recliner. I looked across the room and saw Scriven standing next to my computer. "Leave it alone," I said. Even to my own ears it sounded more like "Reave ih ah own."

It caught his attention. He spun around and glared at me. He hooked his thumbs into his belt and sauntered over to the recliner. He bent over me until his face was about a foot from mine. It was plastered with the kind of grin you see in old pictures of Senator Joe McCarthy.

I heard someone else say, "Smile, Presto."

I recognized the voice. It belonged to Scotty Dunbar, a photographer from the *Monterey Eagle*, the paper I used to work for.

Scriven turned to him. "No pictures!"

That's not the thing to say to Scotty when he's on assignment. He snapped the shutter and sent a flash of lightning streaking through my brain.

I winced. "Ow! Scotty."

Scriven straightened up and gave Scotty the bad eye. "Did you hear what I said?"

Scotty ignored him. He took a pad from his pocket, jotted a note in it, and left the house. Scotty projects a meek-and-mild image with his wire-rim glasses and baggy corduroy jacket, but he's relentless. Once at a fire in Pebble Beach, he kicked out a window at the back of a burning house and entered it. When the firemen broke through the front door, he was crouched in the hallway waiting for them. His ponytail got singed in the process, but he ended up with an AP award for the photograph.

I put my hand to my head to soothe the throbbing and guessed why Scotty hadn't stayed around. He had what he wanted. The side of my face was still wet with blood from the whack Scriven had given me. I laughed, and didn't mind what it did to the inside of my skull.

Scriven scowled. "What's so funny?"

"Police brutality," I said.

"Huh?"

"You heard me, ass-eyes. You can stop posing. The *Eagle*'s got its front page picture for tomorrow."

"You—"

"Knock it off, Ray," Scriven's partner said. He grabbed Scriven's arm and pulled him away from me. The partner was probably in his mid-forties, about ten years older than Scriven. I couldn't tell if he was trying to protect me from Scriven or to protect Scriven from himself.

"You saw he had a knife," Scriven said.

"Don't push it," his partner said, and led him across the room and out the front door.

I couldn't stop myself. I felt my teeth grinding together and a tightness beginning in my head that had nothing to do with getting swatted. I grabbed the arms of the recliner, forced myself to my feet, and lurched across the room. I stepped onto my front steps and yelled, "Scriven, you moron, you forgot to read me my rights!"

Scriven yelled something back about my mother.

The plainclothes cop ushered me back inside, and the other cop closed the door.

CHAPTER 7

They took me to the Pacific Grove police station but—thanks to my neighbors—didn't book me.

Mrs. Banks, from across the street, had seen the redhead get out of a taxi around noon and go up to my place. She'd also seen me park and go into the house around two-thirty. The police showed up a few minutes after I got there, in response to a call from another neighbor, Mrs. Peralta. From her niece, actually—Mrs. Peralta's English was close to nonexistent. She came to the station with the niece, a shy woman in her early twenties.

Mrs. Peralta lived on the top floor of the duplex next to my place. About an hour before I got home, she'd seen a man run out the back door of my cottage and through the woods behind it.

The police sergeant who questioned Mrs. Peralta spoke no Spanish. He relied on the niece's translations.

What did the man look like?

¿Cómo se veía el hombre?

"*Blanco, muy blanco,*" Mrs. Peralta said.

"A white man," said the niece.

How big was he?

¿Qué tan grande era él?

"*Alto,*" said Mrs. Peralta.

"He was big," said the niece.

Heavy?

"No," the niece said. "Not heavy. High ... tall."

The sergeant pointed to me. "Is this the guy?"

"*¿Es ése el hombre?*" the niece said to her aunt.

Mrs. Peralta gave a short, staccato laugh. "*No, no.*" She wiped at her eyes with the tips of her fingers and shook her head. "*Señor Quene no es el hombre muy blanco.*"

The niece shook her head. "You got the wrong white man."

<hr>

The coroner estimated the woman in the shower had been killed around one o'clock. My movements were covered. I was logged in at the library's reference desk for part of the time. For the rest of the time I had Bingham and the Commonwealth Club crowd as witnesses.

As far as the police were concerned, Venus was a stranger who'd come to my house and interrupted a burglary. The burglar had panicked and killed her.

I didn't buy it, but I didn't tell the police that. I didn't know what she'd wanted to see me about, but it had to have something to do with the Windsor Star. Whatever she had on her mind, it was important enough to get her killed. Maybe it was what got Cobb killed. And maybe I was next on the list.

<hr>

Foster Bingham was on the phone when I came into his office. He signaled with a finger he wouldn't be long. I took a seat by one of the windows.

His office looked out on the enclosed flower garden behind the Robert Louis Stevenson House in downtown Monterey. Like the building that housed the Commonwealth Club, the Stevenson House was a two-story adobe. Stevenson never owned it, but he stayed there for a few months in 1879. He worked briefly for the *Monterey Californian*, the local paper that was the forerunner of the *Eagle*. I'm sure they paid him a pittance.

As I waited for Bingham to get off the phone, I took in the view of the garden. It's open to the public, with entrances on both Houston Street and Munras Avenue. The Stevenson House and Bingham's building enclose it on two sides; a six-foot-high wall of adobe bricks encloses it on the other two. Half a dozen benches are set on the rim of the dirt path that circles its center.

In front of the wall directly across from Bingham's picture window, two old guys in raggedy clothing sat together on one of the benches. They jabbered away and passed a paper bag with a bottle in it back and forth. I assumed it contained liquid gold. They could have stepped out of the pages of *Treasure Island*—a pair of hearties from Long John Silver's crew. Their hair was long, their eyes wild. Cutlasses, wooden legs, and eye patches would have completed the picture. But these were no buccaneers, just a couple of homeless guys, out of work, out of luck, and probably out of their minds. They'd hang out in the garden until they were rousted by the cops, or until they finished the bottle and set sail in search of another treasure.

Bingham hung up the phone and swiveled around in his chair. He pointed to the bandage on my forehead. "Nasty."

"Not so bad," I said. "A couple of stitches at Doctors on Duty."

"I heard about you and deputy Scriven." He grinned. "What's on your mind, police brutality?"

"I'd like Scriven to consider that possibility."

"It'd be hard to prove. What with your coming at him with a knife and all."

"Is that what happened?"

"That's what Scriven was saying at the P.G. station—before Lieutenant Schultz told him to shut up."

"You were there?"

"On other business. But when I heard your name, I pricked up my ears."

"What was a deputy sheriff doing in P.G. anyway?"

"He's assigned to that regional drug project—all the area departments are involved with it. He happened to be in your neighborhood when the burglary call came over the radio."

"What about the redhead?"

"They found her purse behind your cottage. The money was gone, but her license was there. They ID'd her from that."

"And?"

"Her name's Tiffany Swift, from Los Angeles. Twenty-four years old. A month ago the Carmel police stopped her for a traffic violation and arrested her for marijuana possession, but the charges were dropped. It was a weak case, and they let her go with a citation for running a stop sign. She was in a rented car, and she claimed the roach in the ashtray must have belonged to the previous renter." He laughed. "It's no wonder she convinced them. She listed her occupation as actress."

"I'm not surprised," I said. "She did a hell of a job on the Nadine Stoughton impersonation."

"What do you mean?"

I took a deep breath. "You got a minute?"

He nodded. "Shoot."

—⁓—

When I finished filling him in, Bingham shook his head. "That is a truly bizarre story."

"It qualifies for one," I said. "Do you know anything more about the dead woman?"

"That's all I could dig up on short notice. A friend at the P.G. department is going to Xerox me a copy of the police report and I'll make a copy for you. I don't know if there'll be much more in it than what I already told you."

"I suppose I should call Nadine," I said. "Save her the trouble of canceling a check."

Bingham shook his head. "You won't reach her today. She called me after the story on Peter Cobb broke and said she was catching a flight back to Boston." He stood up and stuck out his hand. "I enjoyed meeting you, Preston, even if I was the subject of your investigation."

We shook hands, and I said, "I'm sorry your deal fell through."

"Yours too," he said. He looked out the window and I followed his gaze. A cop was escorting the two old pirates out of the courtyard.

"We could be worse off," he said. He turned back to me and gave a dry chuckle. "But, boy, that commission could have been a beauty."

I didn't argue the point.

My driveway was blocked by one of those big PG&E trucks, and a man in a crane basket was pruning the limbs from the Monterey pine in front of my cottage. I made a U-turn and parked across the street from Mrs. Peralta's duplex.

My front door was closed and locked, which I thought a good sign. I unlocked it and went in. The living room looked intact, and I made a beeline for the bathroom. The door was open, as was the shower curtain. There were no surprises in the stall, and I felt a wave of relief. Sounds foolish, but if you've ever found a corpse in your bathroom, you'll understand my state of mind.

My head was beginning to throb again. I swallowed a couple of aspirins and washed them down with a Virgin Mary. In days of yore, I'd loved Bloody Marys. They were one of the few drinks I drank for the taste rather than the kick. Even without the vodka, they were delights.

I relaxed on my recliner and pressed the frosty glass against the bandage on my forehead.

When I was on my second Virgin Mary, someone knocked on the door. I leaned forward in time to avoid spilling it on my shirt, but spattered some on the recliner. Through the pebble-glass window in the door I could see two figures. Glass in hand, I went to the door.

The effectiveness of my "No Evangelists—No Solicitors" sign is limited. It says nothing about cops. The younger one looked like a teenager. He had the kind of pink cheeks you shaved on Monday morning and didn't worry about again until the Friday night record hop.

The other cop looked chronically depressed. She was about thirty, with dark hair, dark eyes, and a creased brow that suggested things weren't going well for her—and would go worse for anybody who tangled with her. Her tone was official but polite. Even before she presented the search warrant, I guessed why they'd come. I should have anticipated it. By now they'd seen Tiffany's record from the Carmel bust. If they thought her visit to my house was drug connected, I couldn't fault their logic.

I let them in and invited them to search away. The woman headed for my bedroom, and the young guy checked out the file cabinet next to my computer desk. I stepped into the kitchen to get a sponge for the spill on my recliner and felt a sense of relief. I didn't like to have people pawing through my possessions, but better these two than Scriven.

My relief was short-lived.

A file cabinet drawer slammed shut, and another squealed open. "Holy cow!" the pink-cheeked cop said. "Will you get a load of this!"

I didn't have to look; my gut gave me all the clues I needed. It was the feeling you get when you rock back on the legs of a chair and almost tip over.

I was already out the back door when the policewoman called from the living room, "Would you come in here, Mr. Kane?"

Not likely.

I vaulted over the fence between Mrs. Peralta's side yard and mine and headed for my car.

CHAPTER 8

I met Nick Allred at my first A.A. meeting, about five years ago. He himself had quit drinking a dozen years earlier. When I introduced myself as Presto Kane, he said, "That your real name?"

I said, "It's actually Preston."

"Well," he said, "if you don't mind, that's what I'll call you. Frankly, Presto Kane sounds like something a magician would put in his radiator—or on his hemorrhoids."

That made me laugh, something I hadn't done for a while.

We hit it off.

Nick's a tough cookie, although his appearance is deceptive. He's of medium height and slight of build, but wiry. Among the more notable physical things about him are his hands. They look like they belong on a much bigger man. They're scarred and calloused—a laborer's hands. He runs his PI agency from behind a computer, but all the work on the small spread he owns above the Carmel Valley is done the old-fashioned way—and by him.

Early in my sobriety, I'd badger him about every little problem that came up. I was a real pain in the ass. But he was patient, gradually letting me realize that part of the benefit of being sober was that I could make better decisions. It was a teacher-student relationship at first, but as he began to cut me slack, our friendship intensified. Rather than looking to him for solutions, I began looking to him for advice. Or suggestions. Something like that.

I was facing tough decisions now, and I'd have to make them on my own, but I knew a talk with Nick could steer me in the right direction.

CHAPTER 9

Nick lives by himself in the Cachagua area of Carmel Valley. He moved there from Pacific Grove six years ago, after his wife died. A lot of people flee L.A. or San Francisco to enjoy the leisurely pace of the Monterey Peninsula. It's paradise to them. To Nick it's a madhouse. His place is more than an hour's drive from Pacific Grove. The last leg of the drive is over rough, winding, dirt roads, but it's worth the jounces and twists. You'll occasionally hear an airplane overhead, but that's it for civilized sounds. At night you'll hear all kinds of uncivilized ones—including the cry of a mountain lion. The first time you hear it, your pulse will get up to training rate fast. Nick describes it as a sound you'd get used to if you worked in a torture chamber.

His kitchen window looks out on a lush mountain meadow, green in winter, golden brown in summer. A spring-fed pool at one end of it stays wet year-round. Deer come there at dusk and dawn to drink. I once saw a mountain lion and her cub there.

Nick doesn't exactly rough it. He's got electricity, a phone, and a killer computer set-up. He refuses to have a TV, but he's got a first-class sound system. His taste in music is pretty specific: traditional New Orleans and Chicago style jazz. It's impossible to reach him on Sunday nights between nine o'clock and midnight. That's when he listens to and tapes a Chicago AM station's "Sunday Stomp," which features his kind of music and through the atmospheric anomalies of powerful AM signals, manages to barrel into this remote region of the Central Coast.

When he does want to rough it, he usually hits the rugged forest and mountain trails a stone's throw from his property. I often hike there, too, both with Nick and by myself. It's a great way to get de-civilized.

———

When I showed up that evening, Nick was getting ready to make supper. He'd just put a kettle of water on the stove for spaghetti and was fixing a salad.

I waved a brace of T-bone steaks at him.

He smiled. He tested the kettle of water with the tip of a finger and said, "Hmm." He lifted the kettle off the stove and dumped it out the kitchen window and into the herb garden at the back of the house. "You get some more greens for the salad," he said. "I'll fire up the grill."

He took the steaks from me and held them aloft. "Looks like dead cow," he said. "They'll do."

———

During dinner and over coffee afterwards I told Nick about the situation as best I could. When I mentioned Bingham, Nick nodded. "I remember him from the Marble Cone fire. He worked on the supply line. He put in something like a sixteen-hour shift without a bitch or a moan. After Betty passed away, he sent me a nice condolence letter. His own wife had died of a heart attack a year earlier. Seemed like a nice guy, once you got past his preppy front."

Nick was familiar with Scriven from the shady business involving the rental of county equipment to the contractor. He had nothing good to say about him. "He looks like a dog poisoner. He's a bully and a sneak—and a coward. The very worst kind of man to give a badge and a gun to."

I didn't offer a rebuttal.

As I wound up my story, I realized how confusing it was.

Nick couldn't make much sense of it either, but he offered a suggestion. "As far as I can see," he said, "you can just step out of it."

"Meaning?"

"Like the philosopher said—do nothing."

"Come on, Nick. A woman was murdered in my house. Some crazy waiter practically killed me. Scriven set me up for a drug bust—"

"Right, right," Nick said, "but I doubt there'll be another murder in your house. And the waiter's not likely to bother you again. All that was tied to the Windsor Star and the Stoughton woman. You're done with her. You're out of the loop. If you need it, I'll get a lawyer to work on the drug thing. That's right up Armand Spaeder's alley—and he owes me a favor or two."

That was encouraging. Spaeder's one of the sharpest lawyers on the Central Coast. Nick once said that if you have Spaeder for your lawyer, it's likely you're guilty—but even more likely you'll get off.

"I'm going fishing in the Sierras for a few days with my daughter and son-in-law," he said. "You can stay here while things cool down. I'll keep in touch."

"How?" I said. Nick owns a cabin in Foresta, an enclave within Yosemite National Park. I'd been his guest there several times. To my dismay—and to his delight—it doesn't have a phone.

"I'll call you from the Visitors Center," he said. "If you're not here, I'll leave a message on the answering machine. You want to contact me, call my number here and leave a message, let me know when you'll be here so we don't have to be playing phone tag. And remember: Keep it simple. That applies to everything, not just the phone business. For now, there's nothing you need to do."

"I'm not sure, Nick. I just don't know what the hell this is all about."

"Of course you don't know," he said. "That's why I have to beat it into your head that there's nothing you have to do about it right now."

I've mentioned what kind of friend Nick's been to me. I don't know if I mentioned that he can also piss me off at times. This was one of them.

"Damn it, Nick," I said, "I want to do *something*. I want to find that waiter and I want to find whoever killed that woman. It's a personal thing."

"Uh-huh. So long as you realize that."

"Well, what would *you* do in my position?"

He leaned back in his chair and clapped his hands together. "Why, hell's bells, boy, I'd try to find the killer and the waiter—maybe they're the same person. And I'd also try to get even with Raymond Scriven. But before you leap into the fray, maybe you'd better consider a little protection."

"Like what?"

He went over to the walnut hutch in the corner of the room and took a holstered pistol and a box of cartridges from the top drawer. He brought them back to the chair and pulled the pistol from the holster. "Smith & Wesson Model 39 Parabellum," he said. "You can just call it a Smith—make you sound like a hard guy." He held it up to catch the light from the window. "Know how to use it?"

"Not well," I said. "I shoot a pistol like old people copulate. No offense intended."

"No offense taken, sonny." He headed for the door. "Come on while there's still light. Gramps is going to teach you a few tricks."

CHAPTER 10

I'm not a bad shot with a rifle. Jamie, my fourteen-year-old brother, introduced me to his Daisy Red Ryder BB gun when I was six. We'd shoot at tin cans in the woods behind our house. If my parents had found out, they'd have had fits. Two years later, Jamie bought me a Davy Crockett fake coonskin hat—like Fess Parker wore on TV—and taught me how to fire his Remington .22 caliber target rifle. Again, we shot at tin cans, but from a greater distance. And again, parental consent played no part in my training.

Years later in basic training at Fort Dix, New Jersey, thanks to Jamie's earlier mentoring, I qualified as an expert with the M14 automatic rifle.

The following week, I took my first crack at pistol shooting. Unfortunately, Jamie never owned a handgun, and my introduction to the U.S. Army's standard sidearm—the Colt M1911 .45 caliber semi-automatic pistol—was a humbling experience.

For most of one morning, we men of Delta Company, 2nd Training Regiment, were briefed on the workings of the Colt .45. We learned its weight, length, muzzle velocity, and the naming of its parts. And we learned how to break it down, clean it up, and put it back together again.

The hands-on part was fun, like doing a puzzle. At least it was fun in terms of basic training pleasures. In the afternoon we fol-lowed a dusty trail to a firing range somewhere in the New Jersey Pine Barrens. There, we took our positions on the firing line and shot at man-size silhouette targets from a distance of thirty feet.

I don't know what the other soldiers were thinking, but I fancied myself a Bogart type. As I blasted away, I wished I had a cigarette dangling from my lips.

After the last pistol report had sounded, the all-clear signal was given. We went to check our targets, our ears ringing. I had gun smoke in my lungs, dust in my eyes, and high hopes in my heart. The hopes faded when I saw my target up close. It was unblemished. I'd missed with all eight rounds. I couldn't believe it. I thought maybe I'd aimed at the target to my right. I turned and saw my buddy, Ar-lander Womack, checking out my target. He'd come up empty too.

A voice on my left said, "Shit."

Another buddy, Paul Youngblood, had also missed everything. The three of us smiled. Ineptness loves company.

I hadn't fired a pistol since that day, so Nick had a virtual virgin to break in. He was equal to the task. "We don't have much time," he said, "so I'm going to show you how bad men did it in the old days."

He handed me the pistol. "You don't have to aim," he said. "Just line up your index finger along the barrel and point it at your target. You squeeze the trigger with your middle finger. Take a squared-off stance and use a two-hand grip, but the main thing is the index finger. Line it up right and you'll be okay."

I wasn't convinced, and the look on my face must have said so.

"Don't sweat it, you self-righteous peckerhead," he said. "You spend enough time pointing your finger at other people; this should be a snap for you."

I didn't need the character evaluation, but I did as he said. As the session progressed, I was pleased with the results. Nick's Smith & Wesson—his Smith—was similar to the Colt .45 I'd shot in the Army. The difference was in the instructor. After twenty minutes or so of practice, I wasn't quite ready for the Olympic trials. Still, I could take a functional stance and point the weapon in the right direction. And I could hit a man-size target from thirty feet.

Nick finished packing his "show-off" car, a new Ford Country Squire station wagon, about eight that evening and left for Walnut Creek. He planned to spend the night there with his daughter and son-in-law. The three of them would get a jump-start on their fishing trip in the morning.

He'd left the keys to his truck with me. "If you have to leave here for anything," he said, "there's no sense showing your own license plate to curious eyes."

It made sense to me. After he left, I set his alarm clock for ten o'clock and grabbed a nap. I had a long night ahead of me.

When you come over Los Laureles Grade from Carmel Valley in the daytime, you get a terrific view of the upper Salinas Valley and the city of Salinas itself. Off to the right is Mount Toro. It's a dwarf by Sierra standards—its peak is about 3,500 feet above sea level—but it's big enough to dominate the northernmost section of the Santa Lucia range.

This area was the setting for Steinbeck's *Pastures of Heaven*—the Spanish called it *Las Pastures del Cielo*—and you can still understand why it once seemed a paradise. Now, though, the real-estate alchemists have begun to work their reverse magic. The golden hills and valleys are giving way to leaden developments.

It was after midnight when I crested the grade. In its own way, the view on a moonlit night is as spectacular as the one you get in the daytime. I could see the lights of Salinas and the upper Salinas Valley stretching as far as the dark slopes of the Gabilan Mountains to the east.

I rolled the window down and caught the smell of sage. I continued down the other side of the grade to Highway 68, the two-lane road that connects the city of Salinas and the Monterey Peninsula. When I hit it, I turned left and headed for Pacific Grove.

Driving that stretch of road during commuting hours can push your patience to the limit. The yellow line tends to stay solid. Get stuck behind a camper with an Ask-Me-About-My-Grandchildren bumper sticker and you're doomed.

That wasn't a problem at this time of night. I kept Nick's pickup truck at a steady fifty-five, cutting through the wisps of fog like the ghost of some ancient highwayman. The truck is a nondescript, ten-year-old Nissan King Cab. Its faded blue body is dappled with gray patches of primer paint. Nick isn't concerned with the truck's looks, but he keeps the engine in top condition.

I'd left my car at his place, covered by a plastic tarp. I didn't know what kind of bulletins or alerts the police might have out on me, but I wasn't going to advertise my presence. I was cleared on the murder charge—I hoped. But I was pretty sure they'd want to talk to me about whatever the two cops had found in my filing cabinet.

I didn't want to talk to them. Not until I'd talked with Armand Spaeder, the lawyer Nick recommended. Nick hadn't been able to reach him before he headed out, but he'd left a message on Spaeder's office answering machine.

I *did* want to talk with Jerry Racker. I didn't know what part—if any—he was playing in this game, but he was the only starting point I could think of.

When I mentioned to Nick earlier that I was stuck, he said, "Remember the Watergate rule: Follow the money."

"There is no money," I said. "The only money involved was in the bidding for the Windsor Star. Now that Cobb's dead, the deal's dead. No deal, no money."

"There's money," Nick said. "I'd sure as hell bet on it. You've got to know where to look. Two people are dead, at least one of them murdered. When bodies begin piling up, there's most always money involved. It's a powerful motivator."

That sounded reasonable. I'd try to pick up the money trail, starting with Racker. If it didn't end with him, I felt sure it paused there.

I'd wanted to call Racker from Nick's, but I'd stuck Nadine's card with the phone numbers on it in my address book. Unfortunately, the address book was back at my cottage.

When you're a school kid, there's a certain face you make in class if you don't want to be called on. No one teaches it to you; it's an innate response. It probably involves an ancient defensive gene we share with chameleons. It's high-level non-involvement, and it kicks in when the teacher scans the room in search of prey. You let your face go super slack, hyper neutral. What you're after is invisibility. When you get it right, the teacher's gaze sweeps right over you, never pausing until it lands on a less-fortunate student.

I tried to do that with my face as I headed down Miles Avenue. I was wearing the straw cowboy hat I keep out at Nick's place, the brim low over my forehead, and Kmart sunglasses with the lenses knocked out. A makeshift disguise, but combined with Nick's pick-up truck, it might do. The chameleon face was an added precaution.

I checked out the parked cars on my block. They looked familiar. All except an old VW bus parked directly across from my place. It could have belonged to somebody visiting one of my neighbors. But it was late, and all the house lights on the block were out. The side curtains of the bus were drawn, which added to my suspicions.

I took a quick look at my cottage. The lights were off, but I continued on. At the end of the block I turned right on Montecito Avenue, and right again on Lincoln Avenue, which runs parallel to mine. I parked halfway up the block in front of the wooded vacant lot directly behind my cottage.

The VW bus with the drawn curtains bothered me. Would the police bother to stake out my house for a simple possession charge? It didn't seem likely. And as far as its curtains being drawn, so what? It seems like the curtains on old VW buses are always drawn. Besides, would cops pick a VW bus for a stakeout? Too wimpy. Maybe borrow a van from a meat-packing company, or use a plumber's truck. Something macho.

Even if cops were staked out in the VW, they wouldn't be able to see me from the street. I needed the address book, and I'd be in and out in less than a minute. Case closed.

I stepped out of Nick's pickup and eased the door shut.

The two cops with the search warrant had followed correct police procedure. They'd locked my back door and secured the inside hook-and-eye latch as well.

I didn't bother with a key. From above the lintel I took an expired credit card that I kept there for those times when I locked myself out of the cottage—which I tended to do. I slipped the card between the door and the frame. With one swipe I slid the lock open and popped the hook from the eye.

A smart burglar could crack the system in no time. But a smart burglar wouldn't bother hitting a place like mine.

Once inside, I closed the door behind me but didn't lock it. I took a step toward the living room, and froze. I've heard of people sensing the presence of someone else in their house. I stood still in the kitchen, wondering if I had that gift.

After half a minute, I hadn't sensed anyone or anything. I checked the living room, bathroom, and bedroom. Empty.

I got down on my hands and knees and crept over to the picture window that fronted the street. A two-piece curtain covered the bottom half of it. I parted it a crack and peeked out. The VW bus looked the same as it had a few minutes earlier.

I scrambled back across the room to my recliner. My address book was under the telephone on the bookshelf. I reached for the phone and stopped. Could the line be bugged? Should I wait and call Racker from a phone booth? Damn. I was thinking like a Nixon co-conspirator. Sometime my capacity for paranoia amazes me.

I grabbed the phone and my address book and scooted over next to my computer. The moonlight streaming through the side window provided enough light for me to make out Racker's number. Besides the regular number, there was an extension.

Nadine had said it was part of Racker's screening process. When you connected with his phone, a recorded voice would ask, "Who's this?" You'd punch in the extension and give your name, and Racker could decide if he wanted to speak to you. I was going to be using Nadine's name. I hoped she was on his A-list.

I finished dialing and heard an odd click.

Was there a tap on my phone?

I'd never know.

The picture window exploded, and the curtain and curtain rod flew into the middle of the room. I huddled against the wall and stared at the twin tongues of fire that flashed from the side windows of the VW bus. My recliner rocked and bounced as the rounds slammed into it. The framed photograph of Yosemite Falls that hung above it crashed to the floor.

The firing stopped, and the chatter of the automatic weapons was replaced by the roar of the engine as the bus pulled away from the curb. The tires squealed when the bus hooked a left at Buena Vista Avenue and headed for David Avenue, two blocks away. The engine roared again as the bus headed uphill on David and finally faded away.

——

Even in the dim moonlight, I could see the recliner was totaled.

Jesus! Talk about being shell-shocked!

My whole world had turned upside down. Dead bodies, violent waiters, hit men attacks, I'm on the lam from the law—and I should worry about second-hand furniture?

What the hell, I'd paid $15 for it at Goodwill. I doubted I'd ever find another at that price.

Total crazy time.

I stuffed the address book in my pocket and hot-footed it out the back door.

CHAPTER 11

The bouncer at Jokers Wild wore a Levi's biker's vest over a red tank top. The outfit gave good play to the collage of tattoos on his massive arms.

"Nice night," I said.

"Yeah," he said. He formed a fist about the size and consistency of a frozen turkey and punched it into the palm of his other hand. "Yeah … yeah … nice night."

The Joke—as locals call it—is the last club you hit before you cross the Monterey-Seaside line. In its previous incarnation it was called The Cave. Back in the day, I'd spent many a closing hour there. Its entrance still looks like the opening to a grotto. Red spotlights playing on the fake rock walls make you feel you're passing through the gates of Hell.

The bouncer didn't look out of place. His jet black hair was worn in a ponytail that reached halfway down his back. He might have been part Samoan or Native American. His nose looked like it had been broken at least once, and he'd picked up a scar that ran from below his right ear to the corner of his mouth. But the battering his face had taken didn't seem to affect his disposition. His grin lit up the night. Some tasty chemicals likely lit the grin.

A sign above the entrance said there was a five-dollar cover charge. It was quarter to two when I got there, fifteen minutes till closing time.

"Waive the cover?" I said.

He tipped his head back and nodded several times, "Yeah … yeah." He gestured with his thumb.

I walked around him—a three-step process—and through the fake-rock opening. A short hallway led to a large, dimly lit room, where a four-piece metal band was blaring away on the bandstand.

The pay phone hung on the hallway wall just before the entrance to the main room. I peeked in. I didn't think any of the patrons would notice me—which is why I chose to call from there. It was safer than calling from a 7-11, Denny's, or other public place where the prying eyes of concerned citizens might take an interest in me.

Safer, but noisier. The band and the patrons were probably powered by the same chemicals that powered the genial bouncer. I longed for the days of closed phone booths.

I punched out Racker's number and pressed the receiver against one ear. I blocked the other with the palm of my hand. The operator told me to drop in more money. I did, and the call rang through.

"Who's this?" a robotic voice said. I hit 343, the code number Nadine had given me.

A second later a woman's voice—a real one—said, "Yes?"

"I'm Preston Kane, calling for Mr. Racker."

"Where did you get this number?"

"From Nadine Stoughton."

"One moment," she said, and put me on hold.

Racker's equivalent of Muzak was Jimmy Hendrix's version of "The Star-Spangled Banner." I held the phone away from my ear and was bombarded by the sounds from the bandstand. Hendrix was better. I jammed the phone against my ear again.

Just after Jimmy's rockets glared red, a man's voice said, "What do you want?"

"My name's Preston Kane," I said. "I'm working for Nadine Stoughton."

"You're the flack."

I'd have preferred another term, but I said, "Yes. As you probably know, I'm writing up something about the sale of the Windsor Star and I wonder—"

"I thought I'd hear from you before now."

"I'd planned to call earlier but something intervened. I wonder if I could stop by and see you."

"How soon can you be here?"

"I'm in Monterey."

"That's an hour and a quarter, hour and a half away. You know how to get here?"

I told him no, and he gave me directions. It was in the heart of the Santa Cruz Mountains, not far from a hippie pottery studio I'd once written an article about for the *San Francisco Examiner* Sunday magazine. Despite its natural beauty, the area has a reputation for creepy Manson-like doings. It's a land where giant sociopaths have, from time to time, roamed free. A hiding place for old bones.

"You'll be checked at the gate," he said. "What kind of car are you driving?"

I described Nick's pickup.

"You're putting me on," he said, and hung up.

The fog made for slow going on Highway 1 to Santa Cruz. When I got there, I picked up Highway 17. It winds through the Santa Cruz Mountains and "over the hill" to San Jose and Silicon Valley. After twenty minutes I turned off 17 onto Summit Road. A few minutes later I turned on to Doe Lane, the private, paved road Racker had mentioned. I wondered whether the Doe referred to anonymity or she-deer.

A few zigs and zags later, I came to the boundary of Racker's estate. The dashboard clock said 3:40.

A guard shack stood in the middle of the road. The word "Oz" was painted above the door. Just beyond the shack, a yellow wooden gate stretched across the roadway.

I stopped next to the shack, and a young guy in a blue rent-a-cop uniform stepped out. He didn't seem surprised to see a visitor showing up at that hour.

"Your name," he said.

"Preston Kane. I have an appointment with Mr. Racker."

"Wait one."

He stepped back into the shack and made a phone call. I looked away, pissed that Racker hadn't left my name at the gate. I didn't stew over it for long. The guard hung up the phone. "You're clear."

He activated the gate and it yawned open. A recorded voice from a speaker said—in perfect Munchkin—"Follow the yellow brick road!"

Like the gate, the brick-paved driveway was painted yellow. It twisted and turned for a couple hundred yards until it opened into a clearing.

Racker's home occupied most of the area. It was a modest dwelling—by the standards of Kuwait's royal family. Even if it weren't a palace out of the Arabian Nights, it would do for a duke, or a doge, or a high-tech rich kid. Built into the hillside, the three-story dwelling looked out across a forested valley. There was nothing man-made in view. Swell digs.

I parked the pickup between a fire-truck-red Maserati and a pearl gray BMW. I left Nick's pistol under the driver's seat. I'd come to talk to Racker, not shoot him. I hoped he had something similar in mind regarding me. If he were responsible for the deaths of Peter Cobb and Tiffany Swift—and the bungled attempt on my life—I could be making a mistake.

Nick had said that when the bodies begin piling up, there's usually money involved. The bill was rising for this business. There had to be at least two people in the VW bus. Maybe another guy to handle the electronics end. However many there were, they were pros. It took know-how to rig my phone. The shooters were no amateurs either. They'd fired within seconds of my dialing Racker's number. And they'd done their jobs. They'd shredded my recliner—with the reasonable expectation that I was sitting in it.

Real pros don't come cheap. But of course, that's relative. Racker had an endless supply of loot. Anything would seem cheap to him, including human life.

I started up the steps, and the front door swung open. The doorman looked to be in his mid-twenties. He wore black Levi's, Doc Marten boots, and a close-fitting white T-shirt that let you know he worked out. Across the chest was emblazoned in red lettering: "DO IT NOW!" He was clean-shaven, and wore his hair cut short enough to please a Marine Corps drill instructor or a Nazi hair stylist.

"This way," he said.

I followed him through a large entry hall and down a corridor lined with framed rock concert posters from the Sixties, all in mint condition. He opened the door at the end of the hallway. "He's giving you fifteen minutes."

I looked at my watch. It was ten to four.

I descended to Racker's den. Racker himself was waiting at the bottom of the stairs, a can of Coke in his hand.

The pictures of Racker I'd seen were misleading. I'd thought of him as a big man. In person he had bulk but not height. I stand a couple of inches shy of six feet, and the top of his head was below my chin. I guessed his weight was in the two-fifty range.

He sported a wisp of a goatee and a ginger-colored caterpillar seemed to be resting over his upper lip. His reddish-brown hair curled over the collar of his white, short-sleeved shirt, which hung outside his khaki pants.

He didn't have a plastic pocket protector in his shirt, but he could have passed for a clerk in an electronics discount store. It boggled the mind to realize he was richer than many American cities.

I extended my hand. "I'm Preston Kane."

Racker's grip was as lackluster as his attire.

"The Stoughton woman sent you."

It was a statement, not a question.

"Not exactly—"

"Well, be exact. You don't have much time." He glanced at a giant digital clock on the wall. It looked like a scuba diver's watch, plastic band and all. It was in the countdown mode. I had a little more than thirteen minutes left. The countdown must have started when I came in the door.

"Ms. Stoughton wants me to do a piece on the sale of the Windsor Star. She said nights are the best time to reach you."

"The only time." He lumbered over to a high-tech chair that dominated the den. He mounted it, sloshing some of his Coke onto the floor. It was a cross between a barber's chair and a jet-fighter cockpit. There were gizmos all over it: knobs, switches, buttons. I was impressed—but then I'm easily impressed by technology. I use a computer for word processing, but how it works is a mystery to me. I assume it's magic.

Racker fiddled with one of the doohickeys on the chair and the seat rose so that his head was higher than mine. That seemed to please him.

A giant video screen was mounted on one wall of the den. It was about twelve by fourteen feet. A horror film was playing on it—a living-dead extravaganza with lots of colorful gore. But the sound in the room was pure Jimmy Hendrix. A blue strip across the bottom of the screen carried a steady stream of stock quotations that juxtaposed with the carnage and the music. As I watched them flow by, I realized I was getting a live-by-satellite briefing on the stock exchange in Frankfurt, Germany.

Racker touched something on the arm of the chair and the channel switched to a soccer game. He hit something else and the Hendrix track cut out. Now I could hear announcers jabbering in Italian.

On the other arm of the chair was a telephone in the form of a bright yellow plastic duck. He turned down the television, picked up the phone, and punched in some numbers. He held it to his ear and spoke into the duck's tail. "Nobody else comes through," he said, and hung up.

I guess the duck phone was supposed to show his zany side. If so—like the Oz shtick—it didn't really work. The stock quotations at the bottom of the screen caught his reality better.

A wet bar was nestled in one corner of the room. The bottles were top shelf: Wild Turkey, Stoli, Glenlivet—that ilk. A right friendly bar. More so than its owner. If I'd been a drinking man, I'd have been offended that he didn't offer me a taste.

"Let's have it," he said, "I don't have all night." He was faced away from me, and even though I was the only person in the room, it wasn't clear he was addressing me.

"I'd like to talk about the Windsor Star."

He pressed something and the chair spun around until he was facing me.

"Oh yes," he said. "The pearl beyond price. Only it's not a pearl is it?" He snickered. "And it's not beyond price anymore. I imagine anyone who wants it could have it for a song."

Sure. Anybody who owned a Fortune 500 company. But I wasn't there to argue economics. "For background, I'd like to find out what spurred your interest in the Windsor Star." That was true. But my motives didn't relate to public relations work.

"That's a moot point," Racker said. "I'm not all that interested now."

"You were interested when your former partner was alive."

His expression gave something away, though I wasn't sure what. "Peter," he said. "Dead Peter Cobb." He hit the arm of the chair again and the soccer game was replaced by an old black-and-white horror movie. I'd seen it before. Boris Karloff played a grave robber in it.

"Too bad you can't ask Peter about that. I'm sure his answer would be much more interesting than mine."

"Maybe so. But I'd still like to hear why you were chasing the Star."

Racker dropped the coy front. "Let me lay out my feelings about Peter Cobb for you. Listen closely; I'm not going to run through it again. When I kicked his ass out of Cobra it wasn't purely for economic reasons. I disliked him intensely. Hated him. And he hated me. I hated him alive, and I hate him dead. End of story."

I nodded, not much impressed with his frankness, since the enmity of the two was common knowledge.

"But you both wanted the Star."

He frowned. "You seem to have a great affection for the obvious."

I glanced at the watch on the wall. It was just passing the eleven-minute mark. Should I waste any more time with this jerk? Maybe it was a dead end. If he wanted to hide anything from me, would he have invited me to his place? Maybe I'd be better off cutting my losses. Tell him to shove it, and head back to Nick's.

A voice from the stairs said, "Jerry, we need to talk."

Racker and I both turned. A young woman in a black leotard, a black T-shirt, and wearing a campy black wig was coming down the stairs. I was startled, although I tried not to show it. Racker seemed indifferent. I recognized the voice. It belonged to the woman I'd talked to when I'd called earlier.

"I didn't know you had company," she said to Racker.

"I do," Racker said, "such as it is."

"Excuse me," she said.

Racker hit the chair arm and it spun him away from her. As soon as he was turned away, she mouthed a word. It might have been "help." I wasn't sure.

She tapped at her wrist and gestured with her head. She mouthed something else, and this time I felt sure she said, "Go."

"I'll talk with you later, Jerry," she said to Racker, and started back up the stairs.

I turned to Racker. He was looking into the bar mirror, and I realized he'd been watching her little mime act. Forget the jolly-fat-man cliché. He looked angry and bitter—and dangerous. His lips were pursed and his eyes were little slits as he watched her reflection climb the stairs.

He turned to me again. "So you want to talk about the Windsor Star, do you?" He was grinning now, but his eyes were still squinted. "It's a pity you're out of time."

He looked up at the jumbo watch on the wall and hit the arm of the chair again. The watch reset to zero.

"No more time," he said. "Go away."

He turned back toward the screen and hit another button. A new sound track came up loud. Much panting and moaning. On the screen a young woman was servicing two men sexually. She looked like she was in her early teens, although maybe it was just the wonder of make-up that gave the illusion. She was no Annette Funicello, despite the Mousketeer ears she was wearing. A cute touch.

Racker was a cute guy.

The stock quotations continued their trek across the bottom of the screen.

I didn't have anything more to say to him. I climbed the stairs, leaving Racker to his high-tech, jerk-off world.

———

When I got back to the pickup, there was a note on the seat: "Meet me just past the gate."

I knew who it was from, and I knew that—despite the black wig—she was the living image of Tiffany Swift—who was definitely not among the living.

CHAPTER 12

I was out of sight of the guard shack and approaching the first cutback on Doe Lane when the Tiffany Swift look-alike dashed from the woods. She stopped in the middle of the road and flailed her arms in the air. She'd ditched the wig, and her red hair glinted in the beams from my headlights.

I hit the brakes and skidded to a halt. She came around to the passenger's side, and I popped up the locking knob and pushed the door open. She scrambled into the cab and yanked it shut.

"Thank you," she said, and gasped for breath.

I put the truck in gear and gunned it out of there. By the time we reached Summit Road she was breathing normally.

"You okay now?" I said.

She turned to me. "Mr. Kane," she said, "we've got to talk."

"That's what you told Racker. Who the hell are you?"

"I'm Tiffany Swift."

"Then who—"

"My twin sister—Jill."

I glanced her way. "The police identified her as Tiffany Swift."

"I know," she said. "That's happened before. She was using my driver's license."

"So who was that at the Larkin?"

"Larkin?"

"The Thomas Larkin Hotel on Cannery Row. The shower, the waiter—"

"I don't know what you're talking about."

"The first time you ever saw me was at Racker's?"

"Yes," she said. "But I talked to you on the phone when you called Jerry."

"What were you doing there?"

She didn't answer.

I stopped at the intersection of Summit Road and Highway 17. Her head was turned away from me and she was breathing heavily.

"Are you all right?" I said.

"I'll be okay." She turned toward me and brushed at her eyes with the back of her hand. "Please listen to me and don't make any judgments until you've heard what I have to say. It's not a … nice story."

I pulled onto the highway and headed back toward Santa Cruz. "I'm listening," I said.

She faced forward and her eyes focused on the dashboard. "Just give me a little time."

"Take as much you want," I said, "we've got a long haul ahead of us."

"Thank you," she said. After a minute or so, her breathing steadied and she began to speak slowly and with little emotion in her voice.

"It started about six months ago, when Jill met Jerry at a party in Pebble Beach. She was up for the weekend from Los Angeles with a guy who was trying to put a movie deal together. He was pitching some moneymen from the Carmel area. She was hoping to get a part in the film, and the guy had promised he'd have something for her if the deal went through."

"She was an actress, too?"

"What do you mean?"

"Aren't you an actress?"

"God, no," she said. "I'm in real estate. Jill is … Jill was the talented one."

She seemed to read something in my look. "It was a real possibility for her," she said, "not just one of those Hollywood fantasies. Jill did theater in L.A.—workshops and actual performances. She did a couple of TV commercials, too. A lot of actresses get their start that way. I'm no expert on theater or acting, but I know she was a first-class actress. Anybody could tell that."

I thought about how Jill had imitated Nadine Stoughton. She'd been good, all right.

"At the party," Tiffany said, "Jill realized the deal was dead. Nothing was going to happen. It was a case of money people flirting with Hollywood, but not risking anything. I guess it isn't all that unusual."

I nodded. I'd been burned in projects involving Hollywood "producers" and local celluloid sniffers. The pitch was always the same: Nobody gets anything up front, *but* …."

"Jerry was at the party," she said. "He had his entourage with him, and he invited Jill to come up to his place and stay for a while. She wasn't wild about going back to L.A. with her producer friend. She knew who Jerry was and she took him up on his offer."

Even in the dim light from the dashboard, the distaste I felt must have been evident on my face.

"Jill wasn't *doing* anything with him," Tiffany said. "Jerry isn't into girls—or boys, for that matter. He watches a lot of dirty movies by himself, and that's it."

The tone of her voice seemed to plead for understanding—whether for Jerry or for her sister I couldn't tell. Maybe for both. I didn't say anything, but it occurred to me that her sister accepted Jerry's offer without having any idea of *what* he was into.

We were coming over the summit now, and at that altitude the sky was clear and sprinkled with stars. Off to the right, the valley was filled with fog.

"After about a week," Tiffany said, "Jill came back to L.A. to pick up her belongings. She told me she'd been hired to work in public relations at Cobra and that it could lead to a movie role. She said Jerry was interested in getting into the business and it could be an opening for her.

"That was the last I saw of her for several months. She'd call me now and then, always hopeful about the movie project. Last week she called and begged me to come up and see her."

"At Racker's?"

"No. She met me at the San Jose airport. That's when she told me she was getting hooked on cocaine. It took me by surprise. I didn't realize how deep she was into it. I knew she took coke at parties now and then. Who doesn't?"

Mother Teresa came to mind, but I kept my mouth shut.

"The movie deal was still in the works," Tiffany said, "but Jill was afraid she wouldn't be able to handle it if she had a bad habit. She'd applied to a private clinic for a detox program and been accepted."

My transition to sobriety had begun in the early morning hours of the day I blew a .26 for the Pacific Grove police. It was my first D.U.I. and my last. When I walked home from the station later that morning I felt a shock of recognition in the form of a question. I had friends and relatives—even my ex-wife—who cared for me, yet I consistently let them down. I'd let myself down, too. Lost jobs, lost friendships, lost opportunities. And the question was: For what?

I went to an A.A. meeting that night and met Nick Allred. As the Beatles said, I got by with a little help from my friends. Actually a lot of help. And with that help and support, I turned my life around. I wasn't sure how people with drug problems got straight. But I knew it was possible.

"A live-in program?"

"Yes. She thought she could get herself together in a couple of weeks. The big thing was, she didn't want Jerry to know about it. There's always coke around for his guests, but he doesn't use it himself. He's actually a prude about it. She was afraid the movie thing would fall through if Jerry knew she was getting a habit. She wanted me to fill in for her until she got straight."

"As Jerry's … housemate?"

"I told you—he isn't into girls." She looked away. "Jerry likes having attractive woman on hand. Decorations for parties or dinners."

"And he wasn't able to tell you two apart?"

"Could you?"

"Maybe. If I'd been living with your sister for the last couple of months."

She made a sound that could have been a laugh. If it was, it had a bitter edge to it. "Jerry lives in his own world. He's a genius in his work, but he's got the social skills of a squid. Lucky for him, he's got the money to survive. He's not cheap, and as long as he keeps doling it out, there'll always be someone around to tell him what a great guy he is. It doesn't matter to him that he's buying their praise, because he doesn't realize it. He's the most unaware person I've ever met."

If she was saying he was a creep, she had my support. But I'd seen the look on his face when he'd watched her in the mirror. I didn't buy the idea he was the stereotype nerd-genius—a brilliant little boy who never grew up. That flash of meanness I saw in the mirror wasn't the only indicator. Hell, you didn't build an operation like Cobra with your head in the sand. And whether he'd done it on his own or picked the right people to do it, his finessing of his late partner would have tickled Machiavelli.

"Jill filled me in on what I had to do," Tiffany said, "which was basically to be on hand in the evenings to go out with Jerry if he was up for dinner, a party, or a trip out of town."

"What about the movie project?"

"We didn't talk about it. Supposedly a decision would be reached by the end of the month. By then Jill would be back on track. She'd been through a program before, and she knew pretty much what it would take."

That didn't jibe with taking coke "at parties now and then." I didn't press it. We were coming down into the flatlands now and were smack in the middle of the fog we'd looked down on earlier. I'd been following the taillights of a truck for the last five minutes, but when it pulled off the highway, I had to navigate on my own. I leaned forward, peering through the fog, reluctantly lightening up on the gas pedal.

"So she didn't finish this latest detox program?"

"Uh, no ...." Tiffany said, dragging out the *no*, as though that would soften its meaning. "In fact, when I called yesterday to see about picking her up, I found she'd checked herself out the day before."

I could understand that. Either Jill felt like she'd kicked, or she felt like she didn't want to kick. But why hadn't she called her sister?

I looked her way. Her chin rested against her chest and I could see she was trying to hold back tears. She brushed at her eyes again. "Today at Jerry's, I heard on the news about … what happened."

"You know she was found at my house."

"Yes. That's why I had to see you. I took your call."

"Right."

"And I had to talk with you. But you never know who's listening in on the phones at Jerry's."

"They're tapped?"

"Not from the outside. It's Jerry's people. He's got a ton of electronic stuff there, including a taping system, monitors, security cameras. There are all kinds of ways to know what's going on. It's just not … safe there."

"You mean physical harm?"

"Not that. At least I don't think so. But it's all about control. That's why I left the way I did."

"Did Jerry know about your sister's death?"

"He may have heard it on the news, but he didn't know there were two of us. And I didn't want him to know. I told him I had to go to Monterey and asked to use one of the cars. He said he'd give me a ride, but he kept finding excuses not to. When you called, I thought that might be my chance."

I couldn't tell how much of her story was true, but I decided to suspend judgment for the time being.

"Do you know why your sister wanted to talk to me?"

"No. I didn't know she knew you."

That seemed reasonable. Why the hell would she? Before I got any more information from her, I'd have to fill her in on what I knew. And so, for the third time in less than twenty-four hours, I related the twisted tale of the fake Nadine Stoughton and the Windsor Star.

By the time I was through, it was close to 4:30. Tiny fingers tugged at my eyelids. I needed a caffeine jolt to keep me going until I could catch some sleep.

I pulled off the highway at the Santa Cruz exit and headed for an all-night pancake house. Despite the hour, the parking lot was half full. Tiffany wasn't hungry. She waited in the truck while I went in to get something to go.

The ambience was orange Formica and bacon fat. The crowd was mixed: fisherman getting a jump on the dawn; hard-party people wrapping up the long day's night; street people nursing their coffee and hanging out until it was warm enough to hit the street, or until they were asked to leave.

I ordered two coffees and two cranberry scones, figuring she might get hungry watching me eat. That wasn't the case. When I came out, her seat was leaning all the way back. She was curled up on it, fast asleep. I ended up eating both scones and drinking both coffees.

When I got to Marina—the northern border of Fort Ord, about ten miles north of Monterey—I turned off Highway 1 onto Reservation Road. There was no sense going through Monterey, even if I'd be on the highway all the way. I'd skirt the fort and approach the Los Laureles Grade from the Salinas side. There was nothing for me on the Monterey Peninsula now but trouble. Maybe I'd be able to fend it off for a while at Nick's place. Much of Tiffany's story bothered me. For instance, how was she able to drop her own life and fill in for her sister on such short notice? But that and other questions would have to wait until I got some sleep.

CHAPTER 13

When I pulled into Nick's place, the sun was cresting the ridge that rose above the east side of the meadow. I turned off the engine and lowered the window. I sat there for a minute or two, listening to the morning come into being. I heard some Steller's jays working out their bird problems. In the distance, a crow called.

Tiffany was still sleeping, curled up on the seat, her head pressed against my hip. Her hair fell forward, partially covering her face. I could see the tip of her nose and her full lips. Her breathing was steady and deep. She looked at peace. Back at Racker's place I'd guessed she was in her mid-twenties, which fit with the age on the driver's license the police found. But lying here now—quiet and vulnerable—she could have passed for a teenager.

I pictured her sister, Jill. How she'd looked coming into the sitting room at the Larkin, the white towel around her head, the terrycloth robe gaping open. And I shivered, thinking of how she'd looked crumpled at the bottom of my shower stall, her vacant eyes staring at the ceiling.

I got out of the truck and eased the door shut. I went around to the passenger's side and opened the door. I shook her gently until she sat up. She rubbed at her eyes and looked about, confused for a moment. And then she smiled.

God, she was beautiful.

"Come on," I said. I helped her out of the truck and guided her to the ranch house. I let us in with my key and locked the door behind us. I took her to Nick's bedroom and aimed her toward the bed. She flopped down on it and within seconds was asleep.

I covered her with a blanket and went back to the living room. Nick's couch faced the fireplace. I sat down on one of its arms and looked out to the meadow. Morning was my favorite time of day here. I stayed like that for a minute or two, letting the fatigue wash over me. I'd been riding a wave of caffeine and adrenaline. Now the wave was crashing. Time for me to do the same. I stripped down to my shorts and stretched out on the couch. I rested my head on a brocaded pillow and pulled an Indian blanket over me.

The next thing I remember was a dream about clinging to the side of a freight car that was barreling through the night in some godforsaken wilderness. A red-eyed beast loped along beside the car. Lion? Bear? Werewolf? I didn't know what kind of monster it was, only that it slobbered and snarled as it tried to sink its fangs into me.

I woke in a sweat, kicked the blanket off, and swung both feet to the floor.

"Bad dream?" Tiffany said. She stood by the stove. She was wearing Nick's bathrobe, and her hair was up, wrapped in a towel. The bathrobe was navy blue and the towel was tan, but those were technicalities. She looked just like her sister had looked when I first laid eyes on her at the Larkin Hotel; the damp ringlets peeking from beneath the towel, the lightly freckled skin, the green eyes—the whole Botticellian enchilada.

I could tell it was late morning by the sunlight through the kitchen window. Tiffany had washed her clothes and hung them on the line that ran from the house to the tool shed. They swayed in the breeze, a feminine touch in Nick's macho retreat. I blinked a few times, sniffed the air. It smelled of freshly brewed coffee and frying sausage.

"Just in time for brunch," Tiffany said. She filled a coffee cup from the pot on the stove and brought it over to me.

"Thanks," I said. I took a sip. It wasn't as feisty as Nick's cowboy coffee, but it would do. "Give me a few minutes and I'll be ready for chow," I said.

"Scrambled eggs and sausage okay, Mr. Kane?"

"Call me Presto," I said. "If you're serving me breakfast, there's no need to be formal."

I took the cup with me to the bathroom. Along with the clothes I keep at Nick's, I also keep a shaving kit and toothbrush. He claims I'm slowly moving my belongings there, gearing up for a complete break from town life. Maybe he's right.

About ten minutes later I emerged, showered, shaved and decked out in a T-shirt and an old pair of walking shorts.

Tiffany had changed into one of Nick's work shirts. The sleeves were rolled up and the shirttail was out, which made sense, since there was nothing to tuck it into. The shirt covered about as much as a shorty nightie would. I didn't complain.

She'd set up our brunch on the deck at the southwest side of the house. A ramada over the deck was fashioned of bamboo poles and split-bamboo matting. Light filtered through it, forming a slatted pattern on the redwood table. It was in the mid-eighties in the sun but ten to fifteen degrees cooler where we sat.

Neither of us spoke much during the meal. At one point Tiffany looked out to the hillside on the south side of the meadow and broke into a smile.

"What is it?" I asked.

"The pale yellow grass, the oaks set against the sky. It's ... it makes me smile to think that I can feel such pleasure at something so simple."

I felt the same.

When we were done, we carried our dishes to the kitchen. She washed, I dried. Our teamwork wasn't perfect. When she passed me the second cup, it slipped from her hand and dropped into the sink.

"Damn it!" She stepped back.

"No problem," I said. "It didn't break."

She took a deep breath and looked me in the eye. "It's not the cup, Presto."

"Hmm?"

"I think we've been straight with each other, but I need to clear something up."

I made another noncommittal mumble.

"It's about my sister's cocaine problem. It wasn't the first time she got strung out. I don't know why I said it was. I guess I didn't want you to think we were … that kind of people."

I didn't say anything.

"There's something else … about what she did with Jerry. I told you there was no sex between them, but that wasn't the whole story. They didn't do anything together, but when he watched his videos and masturbated, he liked to have her watch him."

"She told you that?"

"No. The son of a bitch had made a video of her watching him do it. I don't think she knew he was taping her. But it showed her watching and … ."

I waited again.

"He ran the tape for me—thinking it was me in it. I didn't want to watch it, but it was fascinating, seductive. She had this look on her face that was so … depraved. It was as though he'd pulled her into his dirty little game without her knowing it. The horrible thing was, I felt he was hooking *me*."

She didn't say anything more, but I heard a sniffing and I turned to her. She was facing away from me. I reached out and turned her toward me. Tears trickled down her cheeks.

I pulled her toward me and held her close.

So what do you do? You say dumb things that you hope will make the tears go away, and you wish you could get your hands on the bastard who caused them to flow.

———

The tears went away, and we sat under the ramada in canvas and wood lawn chairs and drank iced tea. The early afternoon heat had put a brake on nature. Even the bees in the herb garden seemed to buzz at half-speed. That was the only sound at Nick's, other than our conversation.

"My sister was tough," Tiffany said. "And I guess I was, too—or had strong survivor instincts. We weren't abused as kids—not physically—and maybe not even neglected. But we missed out on a lot. Our mother died giving birth to us, and we were raised by our father and our grandparents—his parents. He was on the road a lot—a salesman for John Deere, the tractor company.

"Our grandfather wasn't in the best of health. When we were ten, Grandma died, and Grampa couldn't take care of us, so we were farmed out to other relatives."

"You stayed together?"

She hesitated. "At first. My father lived in Los Angeles, but one of his sisters lived in San Luis Obispo, and she agreed to take care of us. She was married, but they didn't have children. They didn't really want us. After a few months she decided she wasn't able to care for us, and we were sent to foster homes."

"Separately?"

She bit at her lower lip. "Yes," she said. "Ideally, siblings should be placed together; however, that's not always possible."

Right. It sounded like a stock phrase from a bureaucrat's manual on dumping unwanted kids.

You hear a lot about the twin relationship. How they can sense moods in one another, communicate in some extrasensory way. I don't know if that's true or not. But I know how rough it can be on any kid when a family shatters into fragments. Maybe it's even rougher on twins. I didn't twant to jab a needle into the open wound, but I had to find out more about Jill.

"You didn't get together again?"

"Oh, yes," she said. "Every summer we spent a week with Father, Jill and I. He'd get a cabin at Big Bear Lake and we'd spend it there."

She was staring out at the meadow now, and I wondered if Nick's place had captured some of those past summers for her.

"Just after we turned eighteen," she said, "our father died in a car accident. Grandpa had died several years earlier, and Father had inherited his house. He wasn't good with money, and by the time it passed on to Jill and me there was a third mortgage on it. Neither of us wanted to live there, so we put it on the market. We sold it and divided about $30,000 between us."

"Did you and Jill reunite?"

"Not right off. I guess we'd been apart too long. We stayed in touch, but she had her life and I had mine."

"She became an actress?"

"Aspiring. She worked as a waitress and belonged to a theater group in West Hollywood. She took drama classes and appeared in some amateur productions. I think I already told you she did some TV ads."

"And you?"

"I used the money to help me through junior college and a year at USC. I was an English major, working part time for a real estate agent. I was planning to be a teacher, until I saw how much money could be made selling houses—even in a sluggish market. I dropped out of school and took up real estate full time."

She shrugged. "And that's my story."

I needed to know more. I said, "How bad was Jill's drug problem?"

"It wasn't good. She traveled with a fast crowd. Supposedly she was going to support herself with the waitressing until she got a break in show business. Her share of the inheritance was going to be a back-up reserve. But she used drugs to keep herself going. Uppers mostly. Coke. Speed. It didn't take her long to zip through her share of the inheritance."

"And she started hitting on you for money."

"How did you—"

"It's par for the course," I said.

She sighed. "I guess so. At first it was twenty or fifty dollars. Then a hundred. Then she needed five-hundred when her engine blew—or so she claimed. On and on. When it hit the $3,000 mark, I called her on it. She broke down and told me what shape she was in. I helped her find a rehab program, and eventually she got back on her feet again."

Her features had been tense earlier. Now they relaxed. The hint of a smile played at her lips. "When she was in rehab, her counselor asked me to come in for one of the sessions. I wasn't interested, but he convinced me it was necessary for her recovery. To my surprise, I found the therapy helped me as much it helped her."

"How?"

"In a lot of ways. Like dealing with my guilt about wishing she was dead."

"Because of her drug use?"

"That was on the surface. I came back for several more sessions. In the course of them we uncovered something from the past that had been a real conflict. A source of resentment—on my part."

"Which was?"

"I told you about living with my aunt in San Luis Obispo. But I didn't tell you all of it—about why we had to leave."

She bit at her lower lip. "It wasn't just that she couldn't take care of us. What happened, she discovered a pearl necklace was missing from her jewelry box. At first, she suspected the girl who came in to clean once a week. But it turned out she had an alibi, and my aunt decided Jill or I had taken the necklace. She and her husband questioned us—grilled us, actually—until we were in tears. But neither of us would admit taking it. Finally, my aunt said she believed us. Maybe a burglar came into the house. Or maybe she'd misplaced the necklace herself.

"A week or so later, our aunt said she couldn't take care of us anymore. That's when we were sent off to separate homes. In the counseling sessions it came out that Jill and I had each been blaming the other for stealing the pearls and getting us kicked out."

"So who took them?"

She gave a short laugh—with no smile to accompany it. "We never found out. The counselor thought our aunt probably had misplaced them and used it—consciously or subconsciously—as an excuse to get rid of an unwanted responsibility. So that's the weird twist. The event that had separated us ended up bringing us closer together."

"When did she finish rehab?"

"Last summer or early fall. Before October, anyway. She got another waitressing job and went back to her acting classes. I was making pretty good money and I forgave her the debt she'd run up with me. I was even able to help her a little from time to time.

"About a month ago she came up with her friend to the Pebble Beach party and ran into Jerry."

"There really was a movie deal in the offing?"

"Yes, but it fell through. That's why she came up here." Tiffany took my hands in hers and squeezed. "Look, I haven't lied to you, but I left some things out last night."

To say the least. "Was she using when she came up here?"

"I doubt it. Until she moved to Jerry's, she'd been going back to her counselor every couple of weeks. In fact, she saw her when she came back to L.A. to get her stuff. She wrote me a couple of times, but didn't call. I didn't talk with her till she called last week and asked me to come up there and help her."

"And you found out she was hooked again."

"Not hooked. She was using. She wasn't on a death trip or anything. I mean, she did have the presence of mind to call me for help. But she needed support—the structure of a program—to get it together again."

Hooked. Using. I didn't want to argue semantics. "So, until she got straight again, you were going to fill her shoes as Jerry's household decoration." I regretted the term as it left my mouth.

She glared at me. "Jesus—you're judgmental."

She was right. But maybe if she'd been more judgmental with her sister—

But maybe what?

There I was again. My head crammed with New England self-righteousness. I couldn't help it. I hated that the life of a young woman had been snuffed out and her sister had to suffer for actions she had nothing to do with.

"I'm sorry, Tiffany. But I need to know more about what brought her up here. Do you know the guy—the producer—who was trying to put a deal together?"

"Cahill. Vince Cahill."

"Do you know where I can reach him?"

"I don't have his phone number, if that's what you mean. But I know where he works—where his business is."

"At a studio?"

"No. He has a car dealership in Van Nuys. Victory Motors—or Cahill's Victory Motors. He's a wannabe producer. Not a rare breed in L.A. Jill introduced us, and I showed him a property in Malibu. He seemed okay. He was in a buyer's mood until the movie deal fell through."

I pulled a business card from my wallet and jotted the name down on the back of it. Should I call from here? No. Better to call from a pay phone in Carmel Valley Village. Maybe I was being paranoid. But I still didn't know how bad the police wanted me. I knew that somebody wanted me out of the way. They'd already tapped my phone, whoever they were. Would they know I'd be out at Nick's? Would the police? They knew that I'd worked for Nick.

I thought of what a Berkeley friend once told me: "Even a paranoiac is sometimes right."

"Sit tight, Tiffany," I said. "I'm going to the Village. If the phone rings, let the answering machine take the message. If it's me, I'll tell you to pick up. Otherwise, don't touch it. I don't think there's anything to worry about, but if for some reason we lose contact, I want you to call this number."

I jotted it down on a slip of paper and handed it to her. "This is Foster Bingham's number. He's the lawyer I told you about. He knows what's happened and you can level with him."

She closed her hand on mine and squeezed. "I'm frightened, Presto."

"Relax," I said. "I'll be back within an hour. I don't think there's going to be a problem. I'm going to offer Mr. Cahill a proposition he can't refuse."

CHAPTER 14

When I got to Carmel Valley Village, I parked on a side street. I didn't think I'd draw attention. Besides the cowboy hat I'd worn the night before, I wore Levi's, a faded work shirt, and my hiking boots.

I passed on using my long-distance card to make the call. Paranoid again? Maybe. But who knows what goes on with the phone company?

Nick keeps spare change in his ashtray. I scooped out a handful and went to an outdoor pay phone. Tiffany had been right. Long-distance information said Vincent Cahill's dealership was listed as Cahill's Victory Motors.

When I got through to the business, the receptionist said Cahill was in conference and wouldn't be out for another hour or so.

"Sorry to hear that," I said. "I'm an investment banker from Carmel and I've got some people here who want to get into the film business. I understand Mr. Cahill has some interesting properties. But if he's busy, I have some other people to call. I'll try get back to him next week."

"One moment, please," she said. "I think the meeting's breaking up."

I said, "Fine."

Ten seconds later a man's voice said, "Vincent Cahill speaking. How can I help you?"

"Hello, Vince," I said, "I'm Conrad Thatcher from the Carmel Valley Investor's Group. We understand you've got film properties we might be interested in."

"Uh, yes," he said, "that might be the case."

His tone was casual, but I could imagine how his heart was going pitty-pat.

"The reason I'm calling, one of our group told us about a meeting you had in Pebble Beach a while back."

There was a pause. "Okay …."

"Well, we liked what we heard. But frankly, we were surprised that Racker pulled out of the project."

"Racker?"

"Jerry Racker. From Cobra."

"I don't know where you got your information. The guy who pulled out was Racker's ex-partner—Peter Cobb."

"Cobb?" I said. My voice must have betrayed my surprise.

"Who did you say you represent?"

"The Carmel Venture Group."

"That's not the name you gave me."

"What's that?" I said. "Hello … something wrong with the connection." I rattled the handset against the side of the booth and dropped it back on the hook.

I put more change into the phone and called Nick's. When the answering machine beeped, I said, "Tiffany, it's me."

I waited for her to pick up the phone. When she didn't, I yelled her name into the receiver several times.

No answer.

I hung up and headed for the truck.

CHAPTER 15

I knew she was gone before I reached Nick's house. The tarp I'd covered my car with was bunched against the side of the barn. The car was nowhere in sight.

What was going on with her? Had she been playing me for a sucker? Was she connected with the craziness at the Larkin Hotel? The murder of her sister? The shootout at my cottage?

I went into the house and headed for the kitchen. I've got a spare key hanging on a nail in Nick's kitchen, in case he ever needs to use the car, or in case I lose my mine. It's happened more than once.

It wasn't there.

Had Tiffany left a note? I gave the house the once-over. No luck.

I was really pissed. When I left for the Village, I said I'd be back in an hour. Had she taken off on her own?

A worse thought struck me. What if bad guys—whoever they were—could have traced me to Nick's? What if they'd come looking for me and found her instead?

None of it added up. Why kidnap her? More likely they'd have lain in wait for me. That gave my belly another jolt. I'd breezed into the house without thinking. Sloppy. I wasn't in a position to breeze in anywhere until I got the bad guys off my case.

I went through the house again, thoroughly this time. The place looked just as it had when I'd left for the Village.

I went back outside and checked the yard for tire marks. I didn't come up with anything useful. I'd put down several sets of tracks with the truck. Whoever took my car made a set, but I couldn't tell if other vehicles had been there recently.

I went back into the house and checked it out again. This time I noticed the red light on Nick's answering machine was blinking. Two calls. I pressed the playback button and heard the call I'd made from the Village. The second call was a hang-up.

Damn. Had that been her?

The phone rang, and I put my hand on the receiver, but didn't pick it up. I waited while Nick's answering machine kicked in. When his greeting was done, the beep sounded and I heard Tiffany's voice. "Presto, if you're there, pick up the phone, I'm—"

"It's me!" I said. "Are you all right?"

"I'm fine. I—"

"Where are you?"

"Carmel. I can't talk now, but wait for me. I'll be there in ten minutes."

"Maybe we should meet somewhere—"

"Have to go now—" She hung up.

So did I, more perplexed than ever. Why did she say she'd be here in ten minutes? Carmel was at least a half hour away.

Would someone else be here in ten minutes?

I wasn't going to hang around to find out.

I went out to the truck and took Nick's pistol from under the seat and his binoculars from the glove compartment.

If company would be here in ten minutes, they'd already be on the dirt road into Nick's place. My best bet was to head for the riverbed east of Nick's. I could hide the truck there and watch the house from the ridge. If Tiffany showed, fine. I'd go back and see her. But if an old VW bus pulled into the yard, I'd head off down the riverbed.

It seemed like a good plan. Before I could put it into effect, I heard a sound coming from beyond the east ridge. Faint as it was, I recognized it.

With the binoculars in one hand and the pistol in the other, I jumped out of the truck and hauled ass toward the tree line. It was fifty or so yards beyond the barn, and as I raced toward it, the monotonous throb of a helicopter's rotors grew louder.

I dropped to the ground in the shadow of a valley oak and shot a look back toward Nick's. A yellow helicopter rose up over the east ridge, hovered there briefly, and made straight for Nick's house. It settled in the driveway and kicked up a dust storm.

I stretched out prone behind a fallen oak limb and brought the binoculars to my eyes. As soon as the helicopter's struts touched down, the pilot cut the engine. Two men popped from the cabin. They both carried rifles. One of them, a tall, skinny guy, rushed toward the back of the house. His shoulder-length hair was platinum blond, his face pale white. He looked like a lanky Q-Tip. An albino! The guy Mrs. Peralta had said was *muy blanco.*

The other man dashed for the shed. When he reached it, he dropped to the ground and took up a position facing the house. From my point of view he was in profile.

Bastard! It was the waiter who'd cold-cocked me at the Larkin.

He leveled his weapon at the house. It looked like some kind of assault rifle.

I rested the glasses on the limb and checked Nick's pistol to make sure there was a round in the chamber. I wouldn't exchange gunfire with them from this distance, but if they came after me, I'd be ready.

I reached for the binoculars, but before I got to them, they flew off the limb, shattering in an explosion of glass and metal. An instant later I heard the sound of automatic weapon fire coming from Nick's.

I looked that way and saw the waiter get to his feet. He looked in my direction, and the albino came around the side of the house and joined him.

One of them must have caught a glint of sun off the lenses of the binoculars. I was glad he was eager. If he'd waited two seconds, I'd have been looking through them when he fired.

Nick's pistol was no match for two automatic rifles, but I knew how to scamper through the woods. I snapped off one round at them and rolled hard to my right. As soon as I came to my feet I was on the move, digging hard for the trail that led to the woods.

The automatic weapons behind me chattered, but they didn't have a clear shot at me—yet.

I took a guess at their tactics. They'd try to bring me to ground and come at me from two sides in a pincer move. My best chance was to scoot straight up the slope and outdistance them. If they gained on me, I'd be in deep trouble when I hit Carver's Ridge, a wide stretch of granite escarpment. I'd be an easy target in the open area.

Once I was over the ridge, I'd be safe. I doubted they'd hiked this area as often as I had. They couldn't possibly know the twists and turns, nooks and crannies I could use to my advantage. It was ambush city. Unless they were complete idiots, they wouldn't follow me into such an obvious trap.

The open stretch was less than fifty yards ahead. Directly in front of me, the path led through a V-shaped gap formed by two lichen-encrusted slabs of granite that tilted away from the trail.

I stopped and looked back. I heard the two men below forcing their way through the chaparral. They were out of sight, but I knew they'd soon break into the clearing. Still, they wouldn't have a shot at me until they'd passed through the gap.

I sprinted off, heading across a level stretch of bare rock that led to the gap. Ten feet from it, I skidded to a halt. My feet slipped out from under me and I hit down hard. I reached back with my left hand to cushion the fall and scraped a quarter-size patch of skin from the heel of it.

A two-foot-high rock was wedged into the bottom of the V-gap.

On top of it, coiled in striking position, was the biggest rattlesnake I'd ever seen.

His overall pattern was a mix of brown and gray, but the underside of his jaw and neck was a startling yellow. He was hissing now and darting out a quivering, black tongue. His vibrating rattles sounded like ice cubes bouncing on a hot grill.

You hear about someone being paralyzed with fear? It happens. I lay there, unable to move. I know my jaw was hanging open, because I could hear myself panting like a dog. The sheer bulk of the creature! When you talk about snakes, you talk about length not girth. How long was this monster? I didn't know. But the section of coil that pressed against the rock looked as thick as my calf.

Shouting from behind jolted me into action. I gripped Nick's pistol with both hands and held it up in front of me. The raw spot on my left hand stung as I lined the sights up on the snake's spear-point head. The barrel wavered. Damn. How could I hit a target like that?

I could try Nick's method.

I aligned my index finger with the barrel and put my middle finger on the trigger. The hell with a head shot. I lowered my aim and pointed my finger directly at the coiled mass of muscle. I squeezed the trigger and the air exploded. The snake flew backwards, as though a hook had jerked it from its roost.

I got to my feet and sprinted forward. I leaped to the top of the rock and paused, frozen. Maybe I'd dealt the snake a fatal blow, but it wasn't giving up gracefully. It quivered and twisted, making convoluted arcs and loops from one side of the passageway to the other. I couldn't tell its head from its tail. I gulped down my fear and dashed forward. I leaped over the coils and entrails that slithered and writhed beneath me.

Clear of the V-gap, I headed across the escarpment. I heard gunfire behind me and the whine of bullets ricocheting off the slabs of rock that formed the V-gap. I scrambled up the last dozen yards of granite, imagining a tattoo of lead ripping up my spine. I reached the crest of the ridge and dove over it. I landed on the other side in a pile of fragmented shale. As I hit, I instinctively favored my injured hand, and took the force of the impact with my right.

The fall jarred the pistol loose, and it skittered across a smooth stretch of rock and over a ledge. I got to my feet, ran to the edge of the drop-off, and looked down. Thirty feet below, at the base of the sheer granite wall, the ground was strewn with rocks, a few approaching boulder size. The pistol was nowhere in sight.

There was no time to look for it. I scooted up to the ridge and peered back across the clear area I'd just crossed. I ducked back. The rattlesnake's death throes hadn't impressed my pursuers. They were halfway up the escarpment.

I started down the trail into the woods, but caught myself up short. I'd never make it. They both had automatic rifles, and I had nothing. They'd shred me before I got halfway to cover.

I racked my brain for options: Give myself up? Bullshit. They weren't taking prisoners.

That was it for options—unless ….

I hurried back toward the top of the ridge. Just before it, I belly-flopped down and rolled under the little outcropping of shale I'd skidded over earlier. It was barely big enough for me to wedge myself into. I pressed back into the crevice, and it occurred to me it would make a nice little hideaway for a rattlesnake. Hooray for imagination.

I fought both fear and adrenaline and tried to stay calm. I breathed in shallow, rapid drafts, knowing that my pulse rate was going off the chart. I hoped the bad guys couldn't hear my heart pounding.

As I waited there—cringed there—I heard a voice from above say, "That son of a bitch!" It sounded like *bee-itch*—a hint of Grand Ole Opry. I thought of Tennessee sharpshooters who could knock the eyes out of a squirrel at ninety yards.

I held my breath.

A spray of sand and pebbles dropped in front of my eyes. The two men had to be standing on the edge of the overhang.

"He can't be far," the other man said. He giggled. "We got him now."

I recognized the giggle. So much for my theory about the waiter being a mute.

The albino said, "Bullshit, Damon. He could be hiding any-where."

"It's worth a look around."

"To you, maybe," the albino said. "We're sitting ducks. I'm going back and check in."

"Okay," the one called Damon said. "I'm just going to take a peek."

I watched as first one foot and then another touched down on the rock plateau in front of me, not eight inches from my face. Da-mon came into view as he moved toward the ledge where I'd lost Nick's pistol.

I eased my hand back and groped into the recess behind me in the faint hope of finding a rock, or stick—or anything that might serve as a weapon. I took a breath and caught the scent of a dry, sour thing that carried a bad memory from my childhood. On my tenth birthday I came across a treasure in my backyard—a dead indigo snake. When I picked it up, something crept up my arm. I flung the snake to the ground, and it landed on its back. Its belly was splayed wide and the opening was crawling with ants. Hours later I could still smell a stench on my fingers that even washing with Lava soap wouldn't remove.

I sent up a prayer: Let that odor be imaginary; let there be a rock here, not a snake.

My fingers pushed into a line of dry leaves and twigs packed into the furthest cranny of my hiding place. My ears amplified the slight rustle of the debris into the warning buzz of a ten-button rattlesnake.

Even when I realized what it actually was, I felt no relief. There was no serpent there—and no rock either. It was the absolute low point in my life. I felt sure these two men were the ones in the VW bus who'd try to kill me earlier. They were still trying. And they were pros. I had no idea what their reasons were. I only knew that I was unarmed and that they had weapons beautifully designed to destroy human life.

In the face of overwhelming despair, there's a natural urge to yield, to surrender. But with luck, the urge to survive can be stronger.

A desperate idea came to me.

I lay on my right side, facing out. With my left hand, I undid my belt buckle and began to draw the belt from the loops. The buckle was made of brass, thick and clunky. I cupped it in my hand so it wouldn't clang against the shale outcropping. When the belt was free, I folded it under the buckle, accordion style.

I slid out of my hiding place and pushed myself up to my knees.

Damon was crouched at the edge of the drop-off, his back to me. He held his rifle in one hand and balanced himself with the other as he peered over the edge. He moved his head in an arc, reading the landscape below.

He stood up and turned my way.

"Snake!" I yelled, and backhanded the belt toward him.

It unfolded in midair and rippled toward his head.

He fended it off with his rifle, and took a half step backwards.

I knelt there, not daring to move, and watched as he teetered at the edge of the drop-off. His arms windmilled briefly, and without a sound, he toppled out of sight.

I spun about, expecting to see the albino. But he was gone. I hopped onto the shelf I'd been under and scrambled to the ridge-line. I peered over in time to see his back vanishing through the V-gap.

I climbed down to the plateau again and went to the edge of the drop-off. Damon—or James, or whatever he called himself—was sprawled face up on the rocks below. Blood issued from the corner of his mouth. His rifle lay a dozen feet from him. From the angle of his neck, I guessed he'd humped his last brunch platter.

For a moment, I felt nauseated. He'd been a human being. Now he was a broken caricature of one. I didn't bemoan his fate long. His was the second corpse I'd seen in the last twenty-four hours. I'd let someone else judge him, but I knew damned well that Jill Swift hadn't deserved to die.

I hesitated. Should I get the waiter's rifle and Nick's pistol? No time. It'd take several minutes to climb down to it. When would the albino start missing his partner?

I picked up my belt and headed down the trail to the wilderness. Once I hit the woods, I'd be safe. The helicopter would be useless in the deep, tree-lined canyons, and I knew the territory well. I'd have the advantage of someone on foot.

An idea came to me as I jogged along a familiar trail. Nick's place wouldn't be safe, and mine was totally out of the question. But if I could get to downtown Carmel before nine o'clock, I might be able to regroup.

CHAPTER 16

The boutiques and art galleries of Carmel-by-the-Sea were closed for the night, but a light still burned in Wicked Wicker, a specialty furniture shop on Dolores Street. I approached it from the opposite side of the street, keeping close to the building fronts.

The permanent window display at Wicked Wicker consists solely of a wicker T-shirt suspended from the ceiling by wires. It's five times the size of a normal T-shirt and lacquered a rich, dark yellow. Black lettering across the chest reads: "My lawyer visited Carmel City Hall, but all I got was this T-shirt."

Whimsy from Tyrell Beaucaire, owner and manager of the shop. I've written ad copy for Ty, and some people in town still think the inscription was my idea. It was Ty's. He'd spent eight months and thousands of dollars in legal fees trying to get his business licensed. Besides wanting to sell traditional wicker furniture, he planned to sell books on wicker art, fabric, lamps with wicker lamp shades, paints, stains, brushes, and other supplies and tools for working with wicker.

He also wanted to sell espresso. On a trip to Italy he'd bought an antique brass espresso machine with an array of valves, gauges, knobs, spouts, steam vents, and other gizmos. A functional art object.

Getting a license seemed a routine business matter, until members of various city bodies muddied the water. Was he going to sell books? He'd need separate approval as a bookstore. Selling lamps? That made it a hardware store. Espresso? Forget it—unless he got a restaurant permit. That, of course, meant getting a special water allocation. Which meant presenting a new application.

"Does it ever end?" he asked me. "Are they hassling me because I'm a black man in a white man's world?"

"It's bureaucracy, not bigotry," I said.

He was skeptical until he heard numerous licensing horror stories from white merchants. "I don't know what's worse," he said, "rednecks or red tape."

With the help of a lawyer from San Francisco, he reached a compromise with the city. He couldn't sell fabric, electrical fittings, or espresso, but he'd be allowed to sell anything made of wicker. And he could serve espresso to his customers, so long as he didn't charge for it.

The compromise was a face-saver for the city and satisfactory to Ty. Still, he needed some payback. Because Carmel's aesthetic posture is based on opposition to vendors of T-shirts and other déclassé products, Ty had an artist create the T-shirt for his window. It got the desired result. At the city council meeting following its installation, a council member put it on record that Ty's wicker T-shirt, "albeit legal, is vengeful and petty."

Ty's comment: "Petty revenge is still revenge."

The curtain on the door was drawn. I hoped it was Ty in the shop. He shared an apartment in San Francisco with his lover, Dominic Mariani, a commercial fisherman. When he closed up Thursday nights, he usually headed for the city for the weekend and left the shop in the hands of his assistant.

I knocked on the door.

"Go away!" boomed a voice.

"Ty, it's Presto."

A moment later the door swung open.

Ty stands a hair over six-foot-seven. His skin is the color of coffee ice cream. To show as much of it as possible he shaves his head. This night he was wearing a white linen suit over a white silk shirt open to just above the navel. The white calfskin cowboy boots he wore pushed him close to the seven-foot mark.

"Something in wicker?" he asked as I stepped into the shop. "Or perhaps you've dropped by to murder me."

"It made the paper?"

"Murder will out, Presto. They didn't name you as a suspect, but they will tomorrow. Believe it. I heard it through the grapevine."

I believed it. Ty seems to have instant access to anything that happens on the Central Coast. His computer modem, fax machine, cellular phone, eyes, and ears were always ready to soak up information.

I needed information—and a few other things.

"I wonder if Dominic's got any clothes laying around your place that I could borrow."

"I doubt they'd be *laying around*," Ty said, "but I'm sure something's available. What else do you need?"

"I could use a car, some walking-around money, and a gun, if you've got one."

"No gun," he said, "but the rest is easy."

He closed up shop and we headed for his Ford Bronco. It was well known around town. Ty's alma mater is the University of Texas at Austin—home of the Texas Longhorn football team. He's a fan, and a set of genuine steer horns are mounted over the Bronco's grille.

—⁓—

Ty's two-story, redwood-shingled house is nestled among Monterey pines, some thirty feet beyond the Carmel city limits. That's by design. He had enough trouble getting his shop approved by the city; he didn't need hassles on the home front.

He parked the Bronco in the carport next to his garage and we followed a flagstone path up to his house. On the way he said, "By the way, I saw Cam the other day."

That threw me, but I tried to sound casual. "You were in Chicago?" I don't know how it sounded to him, but to my ears it was an adolescent squawk.

"Uh-uh, Pacific Grove." He raised an eyebrow. "You didn't know she was back?"

"I've been busy with work," I said. "What's she up to?"

"We didn't talk long," Ty said. "But she asked about you."

"Oh," I said. "What did she say?"

Another squawk. Eager. Desperate. I knew it wouldn't escape Ty. He once said to me, "Your masks are transparent. I'd love to play high-stakes poker with you."

"What did she say?" Ty said. "You know, the usual stuff people say. 'Is Presto still around? How's he doing?' That sort of thing."

I didn't know why Ty was being cagey. Whatever his reasons, I wasn't going to press him. He, Cam, and I had spent a lot of time together. We were an odd trio—odd quartet, when we added Dominic to the mix. We all got along well with one another, and I knew Ty wouldn't let slip anything about me to anyone unless he thought I wanted him to. I knew he felt the same about Cam.

The mention of her name stirred old feelings in me, both emotional and physical. During the months since I'd last seen her, I'd found it easier to block the emotional feelings. I could bury them, reverting to good old New England techniques for disassociation.

It was harder to block the physical feelings. Just the mention of her name brought vivid images to my mind. Cam standing by a stream in the high Sierras, a breeze ruffling her hair. Cam in the morning, stretching, smiling, reaching to touch me, glad that another day was here. A big part of our relationship had been physical, and delightfully so. She was one of the few people outside my family who knew the origin of my nickname. Usually when the subject came up—so to speak—we acted on it.

"She just visiting?" I said.

"Maybe, staying a while," Ty said. "She's house-sitting a place in Pacific Grove, out on Sunset Drive."

"Huh," I said, my eloquence masking nothing.

I'd press him about Cam later. My concern now was making a phone call.

Bingham picked up on the second ring.

"It's Preston," I said. "I told Tiffany Swift—the real one— to call you. She's—"

"I know," Bingham said. "I talked with her. She told me about her sister and Racker and the rest."

"Is she there?"

"No, but she's near. She's safe now. She said to tell you not to worry."

"I wanted to get to your place," I said, "but there's too much heat on me."

"I know. But I think I can get it straightened out."

"I'm staying at—"

"Don't tell me!" Bingham said. He added in a calmer voice, "Let's protect ourselves. I don't want to know anything I don't need to know."

"But—"

"Trust me. Give me a call about ten tomorrow. By then I should have worked something out. I don't think they'll be able to make the dope charge stick. And I think they know how flimsy the murder thing is. They're just trying to keep some leverage. For now the important thing is to stay where you are. Don't show your face."

"I'll be careful," I said.

"At this stage, it's imperative." He paused. "By the way, did Tiffany tell you anything about a diary her sister kept?"

"No. I'd remember if she had. What about it?"

"I don't know whether you know it or not, but Jill was involved with Racker, not just Cobb."

"I found that out," I said. "But not from Tiffany. A guy from L.A. told me. What's the point?"

"I don't know exactly. I only talked with her for about fifteen minutes. But she mentioned that her sister's diary had a lot of dirt in it about Racker. Things Cobb told her. She says it was stashed at Cobb's beach house next to his hot tub, if that means anything to you."

"It doesn't," I said. But that's not what I was thinking.

"For the time being, I wouldn't bet the ranch on anything she says."

"What do you mean?"

He hesitated. "Let's talk about it tomorrow."

I still had the phone to my ear when he hung up. Was there another click between his hanging up and the disconnect tone? Or were my jangled nerves playing tricks on me? Damn. The situation was deteriorating. But at least I now had an idea of what to do next.

As I knew he would, Ty came through like a champ. He offered me his Bronco, the use of his house, and loaned me walking-around money for the next couple of days. It was unconditional, although I could see his curiosity was killing him.

"I don't think your crime spree is just a ploy to hit me up for money," he said. "I think you've got secrets."

"It's on a need-to-know basis, Ty. I don't want to say too much about what I'm doing. If things go wrong, you won't want to know anyway."

His eyebrows shot up. Ty was an information junky. There was nothing he didn't want to know.

"As soon as it's over," I said, "I'll tell all."

"I get an exclusive?"

"Absolutely."

He laughed. "I never doubted it."

"Another thing," I said. "I've got an unlisted number for Cobb but not an address. Any idea where his beach house is?"

"Of course."

I gave him a look.

"I wickered his Carmel house last year. He was so happy with it, he had me do his beach house this spring—from garage to gazebo. I can even give you a blueprint of it. Give me a few minutes, and I'll fire up the computer. He sniffed the air delicately. "And you might want to consider a shower."

I glanced down. My shirt was torn and—like my Levi's—filthy. "I usually wait for Saturday night," I said, "but I guess I can jump the gun."

When I got out of the shower, I found a set of Dominic's clothes laid out for me. The khaki slacks fit fine. The turquoise muscle T-shirt hung on me like a sack. I headed upstairs to Ty's home office. He turned as I entered. "Exquisite timing," he said. He hit a key on his computer, and seconds later his printer spat out a three-color map. It showed a section of the Carmel Highlands and the coastline just south of Carmel.

Ty took the sheet of paper from the tray and marked a circle on it with a highlighter. "That's his beach house." He handed the sheet to me.

He hit some keys again and produced a layout of Cobb's property. "It was patrolled by Rottweilers," he said. "I refused to do any work there until he'd locked the monsters up. But I heard the police took them to the SPCA after his body was found. That was the only security there. As of two months ago he didn't have an electronic system in place."

I examined the layout. It showed a ranch-style house nestled in a gulch and bordered on one side by a small cove.

"Prime property," I said.

"And packed with exquisite wicker work."

I pointed to an octagonal shape on the layout. "The gazebo?"

"Right."

"And this?" I pointed to a small circle next to the house.

"A high-tech hot tub. A 'state-of-the-art dunk,' as Mr. Cobb called it."

"Interesting." I pointed to the scheme of the house. "Got a minute to give me a tour?"

"About a minute," Ty said. "Dominic's waiting for me in San Francisco. We're celebrating three years together."

"Congratulations" I said, and proceeded to grill him about the layout of Cobb's coastal hideaway.

———

Ty started to pull out of the driveway, but stopped and lowered his window.

I went over to his car. "What is it?"

"If I can do anything, you know how to reach me in the city."

"Thanks," I said. "I'll get in touch if I need help."

"Another thing—" He looked at the T-shirt I was wearing and shook his head. "You should work on your pecs."

He powered the window shut, and his forest-green Rolls-Royce Phaeton glided off into the night.

CHAPTER 17

I don't think Peter Cobb had needed Rottweilers for security. His property was protected on three sides by a lush spread of poison oak—Mother Nature's prime plant venom. It belongs to the same family as poison ivy and poison sumac—a family to compare with the Borgias. I first confronted it fifteen years ago, shortly after I switched from East Coast to West Coast. My face swelled so much I could barely open my eyes. After a doctor shot me full of cortisone, my face returned to normal size. I avoid it like … well, like poison.

The beach that stretched in front of Cobb's house was guarded on the north and south sides by rocky promontories. Steep and jagged, they began at the highway and extended seaward for several hundred yards, curving toward each other to form the entrance to the cove. Cobb's house was safe and secure in its own little valley. Unless you had the key to his steel gate on Highway 1—or were immune to poison oak—his place was unapproachable by land.

I'd approach it by sea.

I parked the Bronco at a turnout on Highway 1, a quarter mile south of the gate, and unloaded Dominic's kayak from the roof rack. It was a polyethylene job, about a seventeen-footer. It was bigger than ones I'd paddled around in at Lovers Point in Pacific

Grove. It was designed for rougher water, and I'd have to deal with some to get to Cobb's beach house. I'd also borrowed a dive knife, a flashlight, and one of his wetsuits. The lower portion fit fine. The top hung slack on me.

Ty was right. My pecs needed work.

It took me three or four minutes to haul the kayak down to the water's edge. I launched it and started paddling toward the northern promontory that guarded the cove in front of Cobb's place. It jutted upward in the moonlight like a Spanish galleon, a ghostly relic of the conquistadors.

The seas were running strong. I had to paddle hard, both to move ahead and to keep from capsizing. As the kayak plunged and bucked, cold sheets of seawater stung my face and bare hands.

When I was within fifty yards of the promontory, a wave broke just as I crested it. I struggled to keep the kayak in balance and was swept toward shore on an eddy of white water.

The roar of waves crashing on the rocks grew louder. I plunged my paddle through the froth and pulled with all my strength. I finally broke free of the foaming surf and into the calmer water of the cove, where the waves rose and fell in glassy swells.

In shape, the cove was closer to round than oval. On the side opposite its mouth, there was a stretch of beach about fifty yards wide. I landed there and pulled the kayak up to where the sand gave way to a cultivated lawn. The gazebo stood at the edge of the lawn. It was a hexagonal structure, some twelve feet in diameter. It was open on all six sides except for a yard-high wooden railing. A three-step stairway led up to a hinged gate in the railing. A wicker table in the middle was surrounded by four wicker chairs.

I headed up the sloping lawn to the ranch-style beach house. It stretched halfway across the gulch. The sauna stood to the right of the house, next to a gravel driveway that provided boat-trailer access to the beach.

The hot tub—Cobb's "state-of-the-art dunk"—was midway between the gazebo and the house. I headed for it, keeping a wary eye turned to the house. Were the Rottweilers really at the SPCA? I hoped Ty was right.

A heavy-duty padlock secured the cover to the hot tub. I couldn't see any place near it where Jill could have hidden a diary. Maybe there was no diary. Or maybe I'd picked the wrong hot tub. I decided to check the house. If that didn't pan out, I'd have to find a way to break the padlock.

Another concern: Was Ty right about there being no burglar alarms? I checked the windows and doors for suspicious wiring. Nothing. But that didn't guarantee there wasn't a system in place. Maybe Cobb had rigged the place with space-age laser devices. Nick would have doped it out with a quick once-over. I'd have to trust in luck and Ty's educated guess.

The spring-bolt lock on the door to the deck was like the one at my house—the kind that brings tears of joy to the eyes of burglars. I popped it open with the blade of Dominic's knife.

I left the door open and entered the house. I felt a rush—an intense mix of fear and adrenaline that heightened my senses. Several years back I'd written some grants for New Steps, a halfway-house program that helped people fresh out of jail or prison feel their way back into society. Conrad Dunne, the director of the program, had described that kind of rush to me.

Connie had twice been convicted for burglary, and had served two prison terms before deciding there must be a better way to make a living. He told me, "I never got into heroin, but that jolt when I stepped into somebody else's territory had to be just as good as a hit of smack."

Woolen Indian blankets hung on the redwood paneling. A mobile of jade pieces was suspended from one of the beams that spanned the room. The layout was just as Ty had shown me. The living room opened onto the deck and ran half the width of the house, ending at the double garage on the south end. The kitchen, dining room, a study, two bedrooms, and two bathrooms were separated from the living room by a corridor. Neither bathroom had a "dunk."

Except for the kitchen and bathrooms, the place was carpeted. Through Dominic's rubber booties, it felt like Astroturf. In the moonlight, the shadowy forms of the wicker furniture seemed like mini-structures from a high-tech Stonehenge. Apologies to Ty, but the chairs didn't look all that comfortable.

I checked out the bedrooms and the study. There were no books in the study, but there was a monster sound system and a floor-to-ceiling cabinet of compact discs. By the light of Dominic's flashlight I read a few labels. A lot of heavy metal. About what you'd expect to find in the hideaway-home of a mega-rich teenage surfer. Allowing for a few years, that's what Cobb had been.

A kitchen window looked out to a paved parking area behind the house and an asphalt driveway curved upwards toward the Highway 1 gate. There were no trees on the hillside, only the sea of poison oak that glistened in the moonlight.

I could hear a truck in the distance laboring up a rise and a thought struck me. I could hear the squawking of western gulls outside the house, but there was total silence inside the house. I went to the refrigerator and cracked the door open. The light didn't come on. Had someone shut off the electricity?

Before I could check another fixture, a light came on outside. I moved to the window and froze.

The albino stood on the back steps, a kerosene lantern in one hand, a rifle in the other. I stepped back into the pantry and pressed against the shelves.

Moments later, the albino appeared at the window. He held the lantern up to it and peered into the kitchen. He turned his head from side to side, searching. He moved away from the window. Seconds later, I heard the back door rattle.

I rushed to the living room and through the open door to the deck. I bounded off it and headed for the beach.

The kayak was on the lawn about twenty feet from where I'd left it.

"You lose something?" a voice said.

The albino stepped off the deck, a rifle in one hand, the lantern in the other. "Get over here," he said. "You and me got some business to attend to."

We walked around to the rear of the house. Next to the back steps, a vinyl utility shed was attached to the house. He set the lantern on the steps and pointed toward the shed. "Looks like a tool shed, huh. Maybe garden stuff in there, I don't know. What do you think, partner?"

I didn't answer him.

"Could be all kinds of good shit in there. Duct tape, chisels, loppers, wire, maybe even a blowtorch. Who knows? We best check it out."

He prodded me toward the shed with the barrel of the rifle. "Too bad Damon can't be around to see what's in there. Knowing him, he'd get a real kick out of it. You remember Damon? You met him at that hotel one time. And then again out there in Cachagua."

He slammed the butt of the rifle into my back and I staggered forward.

"Open her up," he said. "I think there might even be a nice surprise in there for you."

I turned to him and he pointed the rifle at my crotch. "You deaf? I said open her up!"

I turned back to the door. It was secured by a hook-and-eye latch. I thought of yanking the hook from the door and slashing it at him. But I knew there was no way I could pull it free. Maybe, though, I could unlatch the door, lure him close to it, and slam it into him. A slim chance for sure, but I sure as hell didn't want to find out what he planned to do with any "good shit" that might be in there.

I lifted the hook till it was almost free of the eye and turned to him again. "Thing won't come out," I said. "Look, it's stuck."

He took two quick steps back and raised the rifle. "Jesus," he said, "how dumb do you think I am?"

I didn't get a chance to answer. The door slammed outward, knocking me onto the back steps and into the lantern. It skidded across the steps and landed in a box of kindling on the other side of them.

And two huge Rottweilers burst from the shed and lunged toward the albino.

Ty had been wrong about the SPCA.

I rolled off the steps and headed for the beach. By the time I got the kayak in the water, the beach house was engulfed in flames. I was halfway across the cove when the screaming finally stopped. I hadn't planned it, but I had no regrets about sharing my nice surprise with the albino.

CHAPTER 18

I drove north on Highway 1, headed for Ty's house. Before I'd gone a mile, I passed a fire truck headed south. I wished them luck. They'd need it. It was too late to save Cobb's place, but maybe they could contain the fire before it spread across the highway and up into the pines and redwoods of the Carmel Highlands.

Just past the intersection of Highway 1 and Carmel Valley Road, I slowed down and moved to the right side of the road. Another set of headlights was coming my way. The vehicle wasn't flashing colored lights, but it was barreling down the hill from Monterey at about eighty miles an hour. As it whooshed past me, I caught a glimpse of the driver.

Scotty Dunbar, my former colleague from the *Eagle*—ace photographer and highway madman. He was hunched forward, peering through his thick glasses at the road ahead, hell-bent on a scoop. I couldn't see the fanatical gleam in his eyes, but I knew it was there.

I watched in my rearview mirror as his taillights vanished from sight. I continued on, glad I no longer had to ride shotgun with him.

It was just shy of two o'clock when I pulled into Ty's yard and parked the Bronco. I unloaded the kayak and went into the house. I was exhausted. I love my sleep, but I'd had damn little of it lately. I'd get what I could—even if it was only a bite-size chunk. I set Ty's alarm clock for six, peeled off Dominic's wetsuit, and crawled into bed.

I slept fitfully, waking at 3:30 and again at five. Each time, I sat up in a panic, because I'd dreamed I was missing an important appointment. With whom and where, I had no idea. I looked at my watch each time, realized it was a dream, and fell back to sleep.

I woke up for good at the sound of chimes. Ty's alarm clock—naturally—wouldn't buzz or ring.

Four hours of sleep is about as satisfying as half an orgasm. But surprisingly, by the time I got out of the shower I was functioning. I grabbed another pair of Dominic's pants and another one of his jumbo T-shirts.

By the time I had a few jolts of coffee it was nearly seven. Bingham had told me to call him at his office about ten. Why wait? I'd catch him earlier—at his house. And no need to phone.

Maybe I was being paranoid again, but I wasn't sure whose side he was on. For that matter, whose side Tiffany was on. The helicopter had arrived within minutes of her call. Had she set me up? If not, why had she said she was calling from Carmel? And had Bingham set me up at Cobb's place?

Bingham had said Tiffany was safe, but wasn't at his house. That didn't mean she hadn't been there. And I remembered the second click when he'd hung up. Could there have been a tap on his phone, or was it my imagination? Could the albino somehow have intercepted my call to him and set a trap at the beach house?

I didn't know who or what to believe.

I finished the last of my coffee and took the cup back to the kitchen. The window over the sink offered a view of Ty's side yard, including the carport. The Bronco was where I'd left it earlier that morning. Only now two sheriff's deputies stood next to it. They were talking with a third man, who was dressed in a green uniform and wearing a Smokey Bear hat.

The three turned my way and I stepped to the side. I watched through the gap between the window sash and the curtain. They started walking toward the flagstone path that led to the front of the house.

Was this about the fire at Cobb's? Maybe someone had seen the Bronco parked on the side of Highway 1 and reported it. If that were the case, they weren't looking for me, they were looking for the registered owner—Ty. There was no way they could connect me with what happened at Cobb's.

On the other hand, if I went to the door, would they recognize me? Were they aware of my problems with the law?

More paranoia? Maybe it was just a routine call—something to do with fire safety. Ty's place, after all, was in a wooded area, and the county had been on fire alert since early summer.

But why the deputies?

The hell with it. It was too early for small talk, anyway.

I grabbed the keys to the Bronco and stepped into the hallway. I ignored the first knock. When they knocked again, I shouted down the hallway, "Who's there?"

"Forestry Department," a voice said.

"Wait one," I said. "Just got out of the shower. Be right with you."

I rushed down the hall to Ty's studio, out the door to the side yard, and over to where the Bronco was parked. I hated to get Ty involved, but it looked like I'd already done that. What the hell? He'd be covered. The way he partied in San Francisco, there'd be plenty of witnesses who'd give him an alibi for last night.

I put the key in the ignition and checked the rearview mirror. Damn. A tan sheriff's car and a dark-green Forestry Department car were blocking the driveway.

The carport was open on both ends. Just beyond the end in front of me the yard sloped downward. A low hedge enclosed the yard on the woods side. If I could get the car in motion, I could roll down the slope and through the hedge. After that the land dropped off sharply through the woods.

If the Bronco could handle it, I'd have a good chance of getting away clean. Once I hit the street at the bottom of the drop-off, it was only a few minutes to the highway.

I put the car in neutral, opened the door, and stepped out. I pushed against the doorframe and the Bronco started to move. When it was almost to the end of the concrete pad, I gave a final push, hopped in, and closed the door.

The momentum carried the Bronco over the lip of the pad and onto the slope. It gathered speed as it rolled downhill, enough to make it over the slight rise at the end of the lawn and into the hedge.

And there it stuck.

But only for a moment. It began to roll back.

I yanked the emergency brake. No chance of a silent getaway now. I glanced in the rearview mirror. The deputies and the forestry officer had a fourth guy with them—Scotty Dunbar. He must have recognized Ty's Bronco last night.

I turned the key and the engine roared. I released the emergency brake, slammed the gear lever into drive, and powered through the hedge.

The drop-off was steeper than I'd anticipated. I shot over the lip, and the front wheels left the ground. When they slammed down, I bounced high off the seat, banging my head against the roof.

I didn't have time to complain. Directly in front of me was a senior citizen in a Bavarian get-up, complete with lederhosen and one of those Alpine hats. He crouched next to a small tree stump, a mushroom in one hand, a canvas bag in the other. He looked up and his mouth fell open. He threw the bag in the air and dropped to the ground behind the stump.

I tromped on the gas and yanked the wheel to the left. My left front tire hit the stump. The Bronco listed to the right and went skimming over the mushroom picker, missing him by inches.

A tall Monterey pine loomed in front of me and I cut the wheel harder to the right. I grazed the tree, knocking off the driver-side mirror as I passed it, and slammed head-on into a smaller tree. I plowed it up and it clung to the underside of the Bronco until I hit level ground just before the street.

Lousy driver? Like hell! If they ever allow Ford Broncos to compete in Formula One races, I'm going to be the new Mario Andretti.

As soon as I touched asphalt, I cut to the right and headed for Highway 1.

I hoped the deputies wouldn't risk county property—and their lives—by following me through the woods. They'd likely take the winding, paved road from Ty's place, which would give me at least a two minute lead. They'd be on the radio fast, but I wasn't going to be on the highway long. I knew a back road route to where I was going.

As far as I could assess my situation, I was now suspected of murder, drug dealing, and arson. And considering the way I'd plowed up that little pine tree, I was probably on the Forestry black list too.

As soon as I'd crested the ridge that separates Monterey from Carmel, I turned off the highway onto the Pacific Grove exit. Midway in the loop that leads back across the highway, I took a right onto Aguajito Road. It's a long, winding road that meanders through the pinewoods south of Monterey until it rejoins the town near the county courthouse. I was bound for *El Rancho de los Lobos*, ancestral home of Foster Bingham. He was a smart cookie. Maybe he could tell me who was trying to kill me.

CHAPTER 19

I followed the hook of Aguajito Road until I came to Monhollan Road. I turned right on it and headed up the hill toward Jacks Peak. Near the top of the first grade I turned right again. Now I was on a rutted dirt road. It wound its way upward through scrubby brush and into the towering Monterey pines that dominated the hillside. After several hundred yards I pulled off to the left and parked the Bronco behind a cluster of twisted manzanita bushes.

No one would find it there, except maybe a jogger stepping off the path to drain his bladder. Whenever I ran Jacks Peak, that stand of manzanita was one of my regular piss stops.

I locked the Bronco and started down to *El Rancho de los Lobos*. To the east of the estate lay a broad slope of pastureland. The sea of yellow grass was splotched with islands of dark green, the foliage of coast live oaks. A dirt road ran between the field and Bingham's property and continued all the way up to Monhollan Road. It was the shortest route to the estate, but I didn't take it. Too much risk of being seen. Instead, I picked my way through the woods behind the estate, stepping gingerly through the poison oak. At last I came to a belt of trimmed lawn about fifteen feet wide. It ran parallel to the eight-foot high adobe wall that encircled *los Lobos*.

The wall, a mottled gray and tan, was capped by red stucco tiles. The face of the wall was weathered and rough. But not rough enough to offer a foothold. I went back to the woods and found a long pine deadfall. I dragged it across the grass and propped it against the adobe wall.

I leaned on it, testing its strength. It would do as a makeshift ladder. I scaled the wall and dropped to the other side.

I landed in the back garden and looked around. It was about ninety feet by sixty feet and dominated by a circular pool at its center. Water poured from the mouths of four three-foot high dolphins that rose up in the middle of the pool. Their green patina matched the lichens that grew on the low granite wall enclosing the pool.

The ground in the garden was hard-packed earth, a mixture of clay and sand. A couple dozen flower-filled oaken barrel halves were set about in a casual arrangement.

The rest of the Monterey Peninsula was still wrapped in fog, but here the early morning sun blessed the garden. An Eden for lovers of gracious living, the wet dream of every real estate agent within fifty miles. This was the last vestige of the land Cyrus Bingham had bought more than a century ago. He'd paid $2,000 for 400 acres. The five-acre parcel—exclusive of the house—would probably bring two, maybe two-and-a-half mil in today's market.

Lucky Bingham.

Bingham sat at a glass-topped, wrought-iron table on a raised patio between the house and the garden. He was in his bathrobe. He sipped from a cup of coffee and leafed through the *Monterey Eagle*.

His back was to me. The splashing of the fountain must have drowned out the sounds of my intrusion.

When I was a few feet from him, I said, "What's new, counselor?"

He jerked his head up from the paper. He didn't turn around, but checked me out in the reflection from the French doors in front of him.

"Early bird," he said.

I took a seat across the table from him. "Yeah," I said. "But I'm getting the shaft, not the worm."

His brow furrowed. "What now?"

"Strangers are trying to kill me."

"Interesting," he said. He turned toward the house and called out, "Anna!"

A middle-aged Latina woman appeared in the doorway.

"Bring another cup, please," he said. He looked at me. "You want a muffin, toast?"

"Coffee's fine," I said.

He nodded to her and said something in Spanish. She disappeared into the house and he turned back to me. "Okay, what happened?"

"What *didn't* happen? But first, where's Tiffany?"

"She's safe."

"You said that on the phone. But where?"

"Back in Los Angeles."

"L.A.! Yesterday you said she was nearby."

I must have looked furious. He raised his hands in a calming gesture. "It was her idea. She didn't want me to tell you until she was safely there."

"The surprises keep on coming," I said. "When did she get there?'

"Late last night. She didn't call me until after I'd talked with you. She was going to fly out of here yesterday afternoon, but she couldn't get a flight. She rented a car and drove down."

"Do you have a number for her?"

He shook his head. "She wasn't going back to her apartment. She's staying with friends until she finds another place."

"You believe that? Yesterday you said you didn't trust her."

"I said that?"

"You said, 'Don't bet the ranch on her'."

"That's what I felt at the time. She hadn't called me as she'd promised. I wasn't aware then that she was driving down to L.A."

"And now?"

"It's not a matter of trust. Let's put it this way: I don't *distrust* her. I can understand her not wanting to hang around Monterey. She's undergone a great deal of stress and she's frightened."

I couldn't argue with that, but it didn't bolster my spirits.

"She said she'd call again in a day or so and leave me a number where we could reach her." He gave me an odd look. "Is there something going on between you two?"

"I've got more important worries than romance."

"Tell me."

"Brace yourself," I said. And I filled him in on yesterday's program of fun and games. I told him about getting Tiffany from Racker's and going to Nick Allred's. I told him about calling Cahill, and about the waiter, the albino, and the Rottweilers.

"Some story," Bingham said. "A saga." He picked up his coffee cup, but set it back in the saucer without sipping from it. He looked off toward the greenery of Jacks Peak and turned back to me. "Preston, I'm partially responsible for getting you into this mess, so I feel an obligation to help you get out of it. But first, I've got to ask something of you."

I nodded.

"Tiffany …" he said. "You're sure she's the sister of the woman they found in your shower?"

"There can't be any doubt of it."

He turned away, drummed his fingers on the tabletop, and turned back to me. "Look, Presto, it's time you leveled with me. I realize that when you were working for Nadine, you had to be cagey—perhaps discreet is a better word—but that's not the situation now. I said I'd help you, and I will. But I'll be goddamned if I'm going to help you if you lie to me."

He leaned forward. "Are you involved with a drug thing—a cocaine thing?"

I laughed. "Hell no," I said. "I don't use *anything*."

He didn't laugh. "I'm not talking about using—I'm talking about dealing. I'm not a criminal lawyer, but I know about this kind of business. The situations you've been involved in are the kinds that happen around drug deals. Big ones. My instincts say that this has nothing to do with the Windsor Star. It's about drugs."

I thought of Jill.

So did Bingham. "Tiffany told me her sister had a history of cocaine abuse."

"So?"

"I'm still not sure why she went to your house."

"I'm not, either," I said. "Unless it was a mistake."

"A mistake!" Bingham stood up. "What kind of damned fool do you take me for?"

"Cool it!" I said, my own anger rising. "I don't mean the rest of the bullshit that's happened was a mistake. I mean her coming to my house could have been a mistake. It had to be something to do with Nadine Stoughton. The only connection I can make between Jill and me has to be through the Windsor Star—I suppose by way of Racker."

As soon as I said it, a thought struck me. Tiffany had dismissed Racker as a rich jerk, a social misfit who had to buy his friends. He didn't use cocaine, but he kept it around for his groupies. So where did he get it? He had to have contacts with drug people, even if it was through his underlings. I took it another step. If he were buying cocaine in volume, would he be paying retail? I doubted it. Maybe he'd bought his own dealership? It was possible. Stranger things can happen when big bucks and cocaine get together. I remembered reading that after ousting Cobb from Cobra, Racker bought his own Learjet. It wasn't a mega-rich man's whim, like buying a Major League Baseball franchise. His accountants said it would be cheaper than schlepping some of his execs around the country on charter or commercial flights. And, of course, it cut down on luggage checks.

"The more I think about it," I said, "the more I wonder about Racker."

"There's also Scriven to consider," Bingham said, his tone calmer.

"That jerk?"

"There's no question he's got it in for you. You said you thought he'd set you up."

"For a possession bust. That's a possibility. But that's harassment. Revenge. Small-time payback from a small-time prick. Murder is something else."

"I doubt he'd want to get involved in murder," Bingham said. "But if he was into something so deep there was no way he could turn back, that's a different story. More than one cop has gone in over his head because of drug money. It's hard to resist, and it's easy to get a piece of the action. And I'm talking about *good* cops."

I laughed—but you wouldn't call it a hearty laugh.

"We know Scriven is dirty," Bingham said. "It's a matter of public record. He's small potatoes, I grant you, but if he had to protect his own interests by jeopardizing yours, what course do you think he'd choose?"

A no-brainer. I didn't bother to answer.

"Look, I'm sorry about blowing up at you," Bingham said. "Maybe this thing *is* a result of a mistake—or mistakes. Maybe the woman came to your house because of something to do with the Windsor Star. Maybe Racker or Scriven—or whoever—had a different take on it. They tied it into their drug thing."

Before we got into it deeper, the Latina woman came out to the porch. She said something in Spanish to Bingham.

He frowned. "Tell them I'll be right there."

He got to his feet. "Come on," he said, gesturing for me to follow him. "Don't panic. It's the police. I don't want them finding you here."

I snapped my head around and looked at the wall I'd come over. No use. I'd scaled it with the help of the tree limb. I'd never make it back the other way.

I looked around in desperation. There was a blue wooden door in the wall. But it was too tempting for burglars. It had to be locked.

Had Bingham told his maid to call the cops? I felt like decking him—but what good would it do?

"Come on," he said again. "This has nothing to do with you—believe me."

I didn't have much choice. Either he was being straight with me or he'd set me up. I followed him into the house.

"You can wait in my bedroom," he said. "Don't make a sound. And don't come out until I tell you the coast is clear."

He hurried me through the oak-paneled dining room and down a low-ceilinged hallway lined with framed photographs and painted portraits of former Binghams. The hallway led to a larger room. I assumed it was the main entry to the house.

There were three doors on each side of the hallway. Midway down it, he opened the second door on the right and pushed me into a bedroom.

"Be quiet now," he said. "I'll see if I can charm them." He gave me a Commonwealth Club wink and closed the door behind me.

I looked around the room. The bed was a high-posted oak affair, covered with a brightly colored spread. The furnishings were austere. A high chest of drawers of some kind of black wood. Another smaller chest of drawers of the same wood with a mirror over it. Two free-standing picture frames were displayed on the smaller chest of drawers. Both held photographs. One showed a man and a woman in their late twenties or early thirties. From the age of the photo and the style of their clothes, I guessed they were Bingham's parents.

The other photo showed Bingham himself and two other men. Actually, the three weren't much more than boys. They were dressed in Army fatigue pants and white T-shirts. They stood in a row, arms over one another's shoulders—a classic GI picture. Although Bingham was probably less than half his present age in the photo, there was no mistaking him. His smile was as striking then as today.

The three looked "young and dumb and full of cum"—as we used to say. There was a palm tree in the background. Vietnam maybe?

I didn't dwell on it. I went to the bedside table and opened the top drawer. Ah, yes. An Army Colt .45, an empty magazine, and a box of shells.

I took the pistol from the drawer and checked it. It held a full magazine. I hefted the pistol in the palm of my hand. The safety was off and I flicked it on.

The door to a walk-in closet was open and suit coats and sport jackets hung from hangars on an eye-level rack on one side. Beneath it, trousers were folded over individual dowels that stuck out from the wall. There must have been a dozen navy blue suits there.

I pulled the light string. Casual clothing hung from a rack on the other side of the closet. I stepped in and took a denim jacket from a hangar. It didn't have an inside pocket and I hung it back on the rack. I took down a tan canvas-and-mesh hunting vest—one of those Banana Republic or L.L. Bean kind of things with lots of pockets, flaps, and metal rings. Who knows what they're for? But it had deep inside pockets, which is what I needed.

It was big on me, which didn't matter. I wasn't going to a fashion show. I stuck the pistol in an inside pocket on one side and the empty magazine and a handful of rounds in a pocket on the other side. I was ready to make my getaway from *El Rancho de los Lobos*, hopefully without shooting anybody or getting shot.

I stiffened as I heard footsteps coming down the hallway. I tiptoed over to the door and pressed my back against the wall. I pulled out the pistol, racked a round into the chamber, and flicked the safety off. I knew I wouldn't shoot a cop—but they didn't know it. If it came down to it, I'd sure as hell try to bluff them.

I held my breath as the steps approached the door. When they continued past, I cracked the door and stared down the hallway. Two cops followed Bingham into the dining room. Neither of them was Scriven. The three passed through the French doors and out to the garden.

I let out my breath.

Other steps approached. They were accompanied by a clinking sound. I opened the door wider and looked out. Anna was carrying a tray with a pot of coffee, two croissants, and two cups on it. If the cops had come to bust me, they were going to get their coffee first.

She glanced my way, gave me a non-committal look, and continued on.

I didn't know why the cops had showed up. Maybe it was a freaky coincidence. Maybe Bingham was seeing if he could work out some kind of deal for me. Anyway I looked at it, there was no need for me to be there. I'd call him or meet with him later—in a safer place.

I headed down the hallway in the direction Anna had come from. The kitchen was on the other side of the hallway. I continued past it and into the entry hall. I kept on going, right out the front door and down the driveway.

I stepped carefully on the crushed rocks. I was walking by the garden wall. Could the crunching be heard by people on the other side? The police car was parked at the end of the driveway. I hadn't heard the two cops when they'd walked up the driveway. I doubted they could hear me now.

Home free, I thought, and stopped short. A man in gray twill work clothes and a tan pith helmet rounded the corner where the wall met the street. He was pushing a red metal wheelbarrow with an oaken barrel-half in it like the ones in the garden.

We met halfway down the path, next to the blue wooden door. He looked to be in his sixties or seventies. Bingham's gardener, I assumed.

"Good morning," I said.

He nodded. "Morning." He pushed the wheelbarrow against the blue door. It was on a spring and it popped wide open.

I looked through the doorway and felt a cold ball of fear in the pit of my stomach. Bingham's back and the back of one of the cops faced me. The other cop was staring right at me. Our eyes didn't have time to lock. As he got to his feet, I was already running down the driveway.

I skidded to a stop at the corner of the driveway. The air was filled with the scratchy sound of radio static. The radio in the police car was on. Son of a bitch! I didn't need to make a decision. As the New Agers might say, the decision made itself.

I rushed to the driver's side of the police car, yanked open the door, and hopped in. The key was in the ignition. I flicked it on and started the engine, popped the lever into drive, and tromped on the gas pedal.

The car fishtailed wildly on the crushed rock, sending a spray of pebbles behind it. I looked in the rearview mirror. One cop stood with his hands at his side, his shoulders slumped. The other shook his fist at me. I was a hundred yards down the hill before I realized why they weren't shooting at me. They weren't wearing their pistol belts. They'd taken them off to better enjoy a *petit déjeuner* with Bingham.

He had indeed charmed them.

Lucky me.

CHAPTER 20

I took Highway 1 north, headed for Santa Cruz. Just before Marina, I spotted a police car headed south. It's cherry light popped on, and I figured the driver had spotted me. I didn't know if it was Monterey PD or not, but it was likely that cops throughout the area had been alerted to my latest caper.

It would take the driver a while to find a spot where the cruiser could cross the meridian and get on my tail. But by then there could be a horde of angry folks after me, and I'd be easy prey on Highway 1.

I took the Del Monte Boulevard off ramp into Marina and kept to the speed limit until I stopped at the traffic light at Reservation Road.

I tried to come up with a plan. Find a car rental place? Take a taxi to Santa Cruz? Or maybe just turn myself in and plead insanity.

The D.A. would have a hard time refuting that.

The driver of a new Porsche convertible solved the problem for me.

He was speeding west on Reservation Road, trying to beat the light. He didn't. He ran it and—his tires squealing—hung a right on Del Monte.

The driver of a pickup truck he'd cut off leaned on the horn. The Porsche driver raised his right hand, middle finger extended.

Vulgar!

I was on him like a wolverine. I hit the siren and took off after him. He ignored the siren and sped up. He zipped through a stop sign, and I did the same. A huge pasture stretched out off to the right, county land leased to a cattle rancher. Halfway to the next entry ramp to Highway 1, the driver pulled off on the side of the road next to a grassy berm. I pulled in behind him. What I'd thought was a passenger riding shotgun was a golf bag.

I took a hand-held bullhorn from a rack on the dashboard and fiddled with it. After a couple of squeaks and squawks, I gave it a try. "Leave the keys in the ignition and exit the vehicle with your hands above your head. Repeat: Put your hands above your head!"

It was strange to hear my own voice amplified. My words were translated into the voice of authority: metallic, uncompromising. I decided that's how I'd play it with this jerk. In the past, I'd run more than a few red lights and cut off more than a few people, but never on purpose. And I hadn't flipped them off. He was also fleeing from lawful authority. Or at least he thought so. Considering my own circumstances, I couldn't hold that against him. Even so, I decided to have a little fun with him.

He got out of the car, his hands raised at shoulder level.

I let him have it again. "Hands above your head—and keep them there! This is your last warning!"

His hands shot upwards.

He was wearing a light-blue Lacoste polo shirt. The armpits went from dry to wet in the time it took me to cross the dozen or so feet to where he stood. I think it had to do with the riot gun I was aiming at his belly. "Over there," I said, waving the gun toward the squad car.

He responded with enthusiasm and I felt a little rush of power—just a tingle. I could see why a prick like Scriven enjoyed being a cop. When the man reached the squad car, he put his hands on the roof and spread his legs wide. He didn't look like a perp—as they say on TV—but he seemed to know the routine.

Only I was following a different routine. "Take your hands off my vehicle," I said.

He stepped away from it and dropped his hands. He quickly realized his error and shot them in the air again.

With my free hand I removed his sunglasses and his cap. "You won't need these where you're going." I tossed them through the open front door onto the passenger's seat.

I opened the back door and nudged him in with the muzzle of the gun. He slid in and I closed the door behind him and checked to make sure it was locked. I got behind the wheel and closed my door. When I put the riot gun in its rack, he leaned forward and pressed his face against the wire screen that separated the front seat from the back.

"What's this all about, officer?" he said. "I'm pretty sure the light was still green—"

"Sir, please remain silent," I said. "Anything you say can and will be used against you in a court of law. Now buckle up. I don't want to get fined because of your carelessness."

When he'd fastened his seat belt, I put the cruiser in reverse and backed up about ten feet. I started forward and cut the wheel hard to the right. I floored it, and the car shot over the berm and skidded down to a muddy patch of land next to a watering trough, disturbing several cows. They mooed their disapproval and went galumphing across the pasture.

I shut off the engine, and the driver asked a reasonable question: "Sir, are you really a police officer?"

I turned my head and gave him a hard look. "That can be used against you, too," I said. "Anything can."

I grabbed the riot gun, the cap, and the sunglasses and got out of the car. I leaned in and gave him a gentler look. "I'm undercover," I said. "This is a sting operation. Drugs, prostitution and much more. If you keep quiet and cooperate, I'll take that into consideration."

I headed back to the berm. I scrambled over it and onto the road. I stomped my feet and shook off the mud I'd picked up along the way. It'd be rude to muck up a spanking new Porsche.

As for my golfing buddy, he'd be fine—maybe a little vexed, but who could blame him? The cruiser was hidden from anyone driving on Del Monte Boulevard. He might be there for a spell. After I'd taken care of business, I'd give the 911 people an anonymous phone call and tell them where to find him.

I slipped in behind the steering wheel and stuck the riot gun in the golf bag, butt end up. I'd never driven a Porsche before. Not that it was ever one of my life goals. Cars don't interest me much, except as a way of getting from here to there. According to Cam, that's a defensive stance. Maybe so.

Nevertheless, I looked forward to grinding and lugging the gears on the Porsche.

I put on the sunglasses and the cap and checked myself out in the rearview mirror. I tugged the brim of the cap lower and smiled at the effect. Sporty.

The ride through the Santa Cruz Mountains was a lot smoother than it had been in Nick's pickup. I was tempted to see what the beauty I was driving could do, but I resisted. I could ill afford to get stopped by the highway patrol.

I turned onto Doe Lane about quarter to ten. I hoped Racker was still up. I slowed down when I neared the guard shack. I waved to the guard and stepped on the gas. I was doing fifty when I hit the wooden gate and sent it bouncing into the underbrush. I headed down the yellow brick road, grinning like a Munchkin.

I checked the rearview mirror. The guard stepped out of the shack and then right back into it. He'd be calling the doorman. I didn't have a problem with that.

The doorman did. He opened the door just as I was coming up the steps. He was the same affable skinhead who'd let me in before. Only not so affable now. He stepped out onto the landing and rubbed his hands together. There was a smirk on his face—that of a self-confident enforcer eager to enforce.

I knew how to fix that. I was holding the riot gun down behind my leg and I whipped it up in his direction. His smirk faded. Magic. If I ever got out of this mess, I was going to get a riot gun of my own.

I gestured with my head and he got the message. He turned around and started back into the house. I followed him. Once inside, I said, "Wait."

We waited.

A moment later, the guard from the shack rushed into the house. He read the scene without any trouble.

I waved the riot gun at him. "Stick close to your pal," I said, "And don't try to get cute."

He took my advice.

The doorman led the way on the same route we'd taken before. At the top of the stairs I heard the sounds of Hendrix. When the three of us reached the playroom, there was Jerry Racker in his high-tech chair.

I didn't stand on ceremony. There was a porn flick playing on the giant TV screen, and I cleared it with one blast from the riot gun.

I stepped toward Racker and jabbed the muzzle of the gun into his belly. It had the desired effect. He looked terrified.

"Why did you send them after me?" I said.

"Send who?" he said. "I didn't send anybody after you. I don't know what you're talking about. Is this Jill's doing?"

I was confused, until it occurred to me that maybe he was on the level. Maybe he didn't know Jill was dead. Maybe he didn't know about Tiffany. My adrenaline had been pumping through me. Now I felt a letdown.

Racker seemed to find my silence threatening. "If Jill told you I had money here, she's crazy. I don't keep it around. And there's no blow here, either—except what's in that bowl."

He gestured toward the wet bar. A pottery container in the shape of Garfield, the comic-strip cat, stood on the end near us. It was about a foot high and garishly painted. Garfield's head served as its cover. The piece looked like it came from a Taiwan schlock factory, second prize on the shelf of a carnival game. Tacky. But if it was even one-tenth full of cocaine, it was definitely a top-shelf item.

"Take it and get out of here," Racker said. "I don't want any trouble."

The doorman took a step toward me. Was he going to try something foolish, or just trying to look good for his boss? Either way it was a bad move. I pointed the riot gun in his direction and he backed off.

"Down on the floor!" I said. "Now!"

He and the gate guard hit the deck.

I pointed the gun at Racker. "You too!"

He slid from his chair and joined the other two, face down on the floor. "Roll over," I said. I nudged him with my foot and he rolled over onto his back. "Let's get one thing straight," I said. "I'm not here for fun and games."

I swung the riot gun at the Garfield bowl, smashing it into pieces and spraying an expensive cloud of white powder about the room. I straddled Racker and pushed the muzzle of the gun into his neck, just under his ear. "What the hell were you and Jill up to at the Larkin Hotel, and skip the bullshit."

"Her idea, man," he said, "not mine. She came to me with the proposal. She saw she had a good thing going and she wanted to make the most of it. Peter had flipped for her. They were shacking up and he wanted to marry her. That's where the Windsor Star came in. It was going to be his engagement gift to her."

"So?"

"So, she said I could set up an auction and start a bidding war against him. It would piss him off no end—and it would cost him millions."

I dug the barrel of the gun a little deeper into his neck. "You expect me to believe that? What would be in it for her?"

"It's true," he said. "She told me she was sick of him, but that he didn't know it. She wanted to jack up the price of the Star. She knew she could get him to pay anything for it if his ego was involved in it. And once he knew I was interested in it, nothing would keep him from buying it."

"He'd spend four million just to piss you off?"

Racker made a sound that was closer to a grunt than a laugh. "Shit—the bidding was going to start at six million."

"So what would you get from it?"

"Satisfaction. After he'd given her the Star, she'd call off the marriage. I'd be able to rub his face in it. Not just the money part, but the fact that I'd been behind it. That I'd suckered him. Believe me, nothing would have given me more pleasure."

"But she'd have to give him back the Star."

"Yeah, but she'd get a kickback from the other end."

That caught me off guard. "From Nadine Stoughton?"

"Somebody on that end."

Who else could it be? Bingham? Maybe. But it didn't seem to fit with what I'd dug up so far. What about Lew Stiles—the Boston lawyer who'd put Nadine in touch with Bingham? I couldn't even guess at that one. The fact was, they were all possibilities. Bingham, Stiles, Nadine. Any one of them could have started this weird ball rolling.

Another piece didn't fit into the puzzle. I poked Racker's belly with the riot gun. "How could Jill have been living here with you and with Cobb in Pebble Beach at the same time?"

"She wasn't living here," he said. "She stayed a few nights. She told Peter she had to go back to L.A. because her sister was recovering from an operation."

That didn't fit with what Tiffany had told me. But then she'd gotten her information from her sister.

"What about the business at the Hotel Larkin?"

"That was me," he said. "I set it up. Jill knew the Stoughton woman was going to be staying there, so I reserved a suite near hers and had her phone bugged. I wanted to be on top of the situation until I was sure Peter would swallow the bait."

"The desk clerk said the other suite was empty." I gave the barrel another wiggle.

"Of course he did. I paid him enough."

An image of that weasel with his *GQ* magazine and smarmy smile flashed through my mind. I'd deal with him later.

"Why did Jill call me and set up the interview at the Larkin?"

"To divert you." He nodded toward the gate guard. "While you were talking with her, Everett was supposed to see the Stoughton woman, pretending to be you. He's an actor, too. He was going to get me more inside information about the bidding arrangements."

I looked at the gate guard. He turned his head to look up at me and raised his eyebrows. He came as close to shrugging as someone lying belly down on a floor could.

I turned back to Racker. "So why didn't he?"

"Because before you got there I heard on the radio that they'd found Peter's body. That meant there'd be no bidding. We didn't need to divert you."

"But you let Jill go through with the whole process anyway."

His brow wrinkled. "I don't know what you're talking about. As soon as I heard Peter was dead, I called Everett and Jill and told them to shut the operation down."

"What about the waiter who slugged me?"

Racker looked bewildered. "I don't know what you're talking about."

There was enough defiance in his tone to make me believe him.

"And I don't know why you're making such a big thing out of it," he said. "It was just a game between Peter and me. Now he's dead and it's over. Nobody got hurt."

I felt a strong urge to a blast his kneecaps. But then, he didn't know about Jill. And, of course, he didn't know about the other corpses that were accumulating.

"Okay, pervert," I said "pay attention; I'm not going to repeat myself. Jill's seventeen years old. I don't know everything you did with her, but she's got taped and photo evidence that you had drugs and pornography on the premises. She's a minor, and that's enough to get you prison time and a permanent sex-offender rap sheet. If you ever try to hurt her—or even get in touch with her in any way—you're going down." I looked at the other two. "All of you!"

I don't know if Racker believed me or if it was the riot gun that put the terrified look on his face. I didn't care.

I stepped back and glanced at the workbench in the corner. There was a roll of duct tape on it and I thought about binding them with it. But I didn't think he'd be calling the cops. At least not until they got the cocaine cleaned up. Not even then. Anyway you looked at it, he'd be happy to have me out of there.

I turned to the stairs and heard a quacking sound behind me. I spun around and swung the riot gun in that direction. Racker's yellow-duck telephone sat next to his high-tech chair.

"I hate that cute shit," I said. I put the muzzle against the duck's breast. When it quacked again, I pulled the trigger.

I turned back to Racker. "Get a real phone," I said, and left the Land of Oz.

⁓

On the drive back to the Monterey Peninsula, I was still in the dark about the whole damned mess. But at least I'd eliminated Jerry Racker as a suspect. Now I had to find out where Vincent Cahill and Raymond Scriven fit in.

CHAPTER 21

In the early afternoon light, the entrance to Jokers Wild didn't look so hellish. Tawdry maybe, but since it was my home-office-away-from-home, I wasn't going to bitch about it.

There was no bouncer on duty. My pal was probably nestled snug in his bed, resting up for the night's work ahead. Or—just as likely—loading up on crank with some of his cronies.

On the drive down from Santa Cruz, I'd done some thinking about Raymond Scriven. First off, I didn't think he was pulling the strings. He was too dumb for that. He was a crook, but he was also a bonehead. The equipment-rental scam was a good example. Did it take a genius to know someone would notice a city bulldozer was working a private job? And pistol-whipping me when there was a news photographer standing by was another brilliant move. No, if he were involved in this thing, it'd be at a low level. Still, I might be able to use him as a link to whoever *was* behind it.

He hadn't been out at Nick's with the albino and the waiter—unless he'd been flying the helicopter. But I didn't think he was a pilot. Nor did I think he was at Cobb's when the albino went full-Alpo. But he could have been in on the gunfire barrage at my cottage. As Bingham had said, the attack looked like a drug hit.

But why would drug people be after me?

It didn't make sense. Unless you approached it from another angle. Maybe it was meant to look like a drug hit, to give someone else cover. I was sure Scriven had set me up for the drug bust earlier. He could have done it on the spur of the moment, or it could have been part of a bigger plan.

The more I thought about it, the more likely it seemed that Scriven was involved. It fit his character. Lying in wait in the dark of night. And as a cop, he probably knew how to get his hands on automatic weapons. If I'd been killed, it would have been chalked up to a drug deal gone bad. Jill Swift's murder would be laid off on the same people who did me.

But why Jill Swift? And to voice the universal complaint—why me?

It had to be tied to the Windsor Star, but how? For now I could work on two small pieces. I could find out where Scriven was when my place was hit. And I could find out if he knew how to pilot a helicopter.

⸻

I dropped some change in the phone and dialed Patti Delgado's work number at Monterey City Hall. She's now the head computer maven for the Planning Commission. I first met her when I was a reporter for the *Eagle*. She's a hard worker and a hard partier. She'd helped me out on a number of stories when my beat was city hall. I hoped she could help me now.

As soon as she answered, I said, "Patti, I need a favor."

She recognized my voice. "Sure, Presto," she said. "Bail? A jailbreak? A pardon?"

"I guess you've seen the paper."

"Heard it on KAZU. What can I do for you?"

"I need some information from the sheriff's office, Patti. And with your contacts—"

"Cut the soft soap, Presto."

"Okay," I said. "This thing's nothing heavy. I just need to check out a duty roster for Tuesday night."

She hesitated. "This better be important."

"It is," I said. "I need to know where someone from the sheriff's office was Tuesday night."

"Your old friend Scriven?"

"Uh-huh. Can you do it?"

"Done and done," she said. "He wasn't on duty—but I know where he was."

Patti is efficient, but this was amazing. "You're already in the sheriff's computer?"

"That's impossible, Presto. And even if it were possible, it'd be illegal. You should know better. But I was at our city council meeting Tuesday night, and so was Scriven and a delegation of other people from the sheriff's department. The county is considering aligning their pay scale with the Monterey PD. It was the last item on the agenda and they didn't finish until after midnight."

"He was there the whole time?"

"And not happy about it. You've covered enough council meetings to know how boring they can be. That one was no exception."

"But he left just after midnight?"

"Everybody did. And most of us went to New Monterey and closed Segovia's. Who wouldn't after a night like that?" She paused. "*You* wouldn't now, of course. But in days gone by, you'd be—"

"Patti," I said, "was Scriven there too?"

"Naturally. Besides being dumb and vicious, he's a drunk and a loudmouth. If he didn't have a badge, they'd have 86ed his ass from Segovia's ten minutes after he got there."

I greeted the news with mixed feelings. I wanted Scriven to have been involved in the attack at my house. It would simplify the situation, give me a demon I could recognize. But he wasn't off the hook for the attack at Nick's place. I hoped my next call would clarify that.

I thanked Patti profusely and promised I'd take her to dinner soon at Club XIX in Pebble Beach.

"Wonderful," she said. "If you're not making license plates in Folsom."

I fed the phone slot again and dialed a familiar number.

"Newsroom," a voice said. "Dan Sheldon speaking."

"Danny," I said, "it's Presto."

"All right!" he said. "The desperado."

"I need some information."

"Fire away."

"You did a piece on Raymond Scriven during that rental thing."

"Yeah. He who protects and serves. Rumor says you exchanged cross words with him recently."

"Things got a bit testy."

Danny chuckled. "I heard you called him 'ass-eyes.' Nice turn of phrase."

"Thanks," I said. I could imagine Danny sitting in his cubicle, his feet up on the desk, happy to be distracted from deadlines and other annoyances of the job. At any other time, I'd have enjoyed chatting with him. Now I was in a hurry. "Danny," I said, "do you remember anything about his ever flying a helicopter."

"Uh-uh."

"In the service maybe?"

"No. I went through his records with a microscope. He was in the Army—Military Police. I remember thinking he must have been a real prick as an MP—just like he is as a cop."

"Nothing about flying?"

"I can check in the morgue for anything we published. I don't have my notes handy, but I'm pretty sure there was nothing about him flying."

That satisfied me. Danny was a pro.

I said, "Thanks."

"No problem. By the way, are you going to turn yourself in?"

"When I do, I'll call you. There should be a Pulitzer in it for you."

I hung up the phone. Damn. That pretty much ruled Scriven out, but it didn't rule anyone else in.

I went to the bar to get change for my next call. When I returned, a liquor salesman was using the phone. I went back to the bar and ordered a Virgin Mary. Someone had left a copy of the *San Jose Mercury-News* there, and I leafed through it while I waited for the salesman to finish his call.

In the second section there was a follow-up story on Peter Cobb's death. The coroner had ruled out accidental death. Cobb hadn't died from drowning; he'd been strangled. I thought of Jill Swift and the bruises on her neck.

There was another reference to his death in the business section. Mongoose stock was plummeting. It had been hovering around twenty-eight dollars a share early in the week. Before they took it off the market it was down to around five dollars. That would please Racker, even though he couldn't rub Cobb's nose in it.

The salesman must have been talking with his girlfriend. By the time he finished his call, I was catching up on middle-school soccer scores. I hurried to the phone and rattled out a handful of change on the metal shelf.

Hell hath no fury like a Hollywood hopeful scorned. Peter Cobb had stiffed Vincent Cahill on a movie deal. Was that enough motivation for Cahill to turn Cobb into a stiff?

I knew it was farfetched—but I was desperate. Even if Cahill wasn't the man behind the plan, I still wanted to talk with him again. He was the only Los Angeles link I had to Tiffany. He'd met her through Jill, and there was an outside chance he'd know where she was.

This time when I called the car dealership, I didn't play coy games about investment bankers from Carmel.

"Cahill's Victory Motors," the receptionist said.

"This is Lieutenant Edward Phelan of the Los Angeles Police Department," I said. "I need to speak with Mr. Cahill about an urgent matter."

"Yes, Lieutenant," she said. "Just a moment, please."

Seconds later, Cahill was on the line. "What's this all about?"

"Mr. Cahill," I said, "we're trying to locate a young woman who may have worked for you in the past."

"Who's that?"

"Tiffany Swift."

"No—I don't remember any Tiffany. What was she supposed to have done here?"

I ignored his question. "She might have used the name Jill Swift."

"That bitch!" he said. "She never worked for me. She was a little scam artist who tried to hustle me out of—"

He paused. "Who did you say you were?"

"Lieutenant Phelan, LAPD."

"Yeah, bullshit! I know who you are. You called before."

Damn. That was the problem with having a distinctive New England accent.

"If you're calling for Foster Bingham," he said, his voice rising, "forget it! I don't owe him a goddamned cent. And if he wants to tangle assholes with me, you tell him that's just fine. I've got a couple of Beverly Hills lawyers who'll kick his hayseed ass from here to Timbuktu."

He slammed down the receiver.

By then I was holding my receiver away from my ear, so it wasn't all that jarring. But that doesn't mean I wasn't shocked. A whole new picture was developing. Cahill hadn't been putting on an act. He was genuinely pissed off. He didn't know where Tiffany was— or about Jill's death. But he knew Bingham—by name, anyway. And maybe by reputation.

Foster "Binx" Bingham. Public-spirited citizen. Commonwealth Club hotshot. Volunteer firefighter. Army veteran.

I thought about the photo of Bingham and his army buddies.

And I thought about Fort Rucker.

Damn! Why hadn't I thought about it earlier?

I headed out to my purloined Porsche.

———

I parked in the small lot behind the library and went in through the rear door. Business was slow. A handful of adults sat at the tables in the periodicals section. A half-dozen summer school students from the high school just up the street sat at a table near the reference desk. Two of them were absorbed in their books. The other four were giggling and chattering away in whispers—soft enough not to be understood, but loud enough to annoy the scattering of older patrons.

I walked behind the wood and stained glass partition that separated the reference section from the library's main entrance. A young librarian was shelving a book there. I recognized her, but didn't know her by name. "Excuse me," I said. "Do you know if Bill Kittering's here today?"

"He's on his break," she said. "Can I help you?"

I needed to get into the California Room, but I didn't need to give my name to someone I didn't know. "That's okay," I said. "I'll check back later."

She gave me a funny look. "Suit yourself," she said.

———

I rushed up the stairs, hoping the California Room was unlocked. It was. And Robin Hood's granny—bless her heart—was sleeping at the helm again.

I went to the "B" drawer and removed Foster Bingham's file. The most recent entry was a clip from the *Eagle* pasted onto a sheet of bond paper, a photo of Bingham and the president of a local bank. They were each holding one end of a huge facsimile of a check for $5,000 that had been donated to the local YWCA on behalf of The Bing Crosby National Pro-Am.

There were a number of similar clips: Bingham posing with members of Rotary, the Chamber of Commerce, the American Legion, the VFW, the Buddy Program, and so on. In some he was accepting checks for nonprofits; in others he was giving them out.

I finally found what I was looking for. A yellowed newspaper photo that had been taken about the same time the one in his bedroom was taken. He was wearing his Class A uniform and smiling as a colonel pinned something to his chest.

The caption read: "Warrant Officer Foster Bingham of Monterey receives his wings from Col. William Stanley. A graduate of Monterey High School and Stanford University, Bingham recently finished first in his class at the U.S. Army Helicopter School at Fort Rucker, Alabama."

I slammed the drawer shut, stormed out of the California Room, and headed for the mezzanine pay phone.

Nick's answering machine answered on the second ring. As soon as his greeting came on I pressed seven and waited for the messages to play back.

There was only one. It was from Tiffany.

"Presto, it's me," she said. "If you're there, please pick up. I've tried to reach you, but I keep getting the answering machine. I didn't want to leave a message. Now I don't have a choice. I'm on the way to Nick's place. I'll be there in an hour."

She hung up. The machine told me the call was recorded at 3:22 p.m. Friday. I looked at my watch. It was now 4:15.

I had to get to Nick's before Bingham did.

CHAPTER 22

I hung up the phone and headed for the stairs. I was about to start down when I saw two cops at the reference desk. The woman with the wrinkled brow and the pink-cheeked guy who'd found the stash at my house.

Damn! That explained the funny look the librarian had given me. She pointed at me and said something to the cops.

The young one turned toward me. "You!" he said. "Don't move!"

Forget it. I was already moving.

He and his partner rushed for the stairs.

A pair of teenage sweethearts were pawing each other at a maple table near the staircase.

"Excuse me," I said. I grabbed the edge of the table, yanked it away from them, and dragged it to the top of the stairs. The cops were halfway up the stairs, and I upended the table and sent it tumbling toward them.

They jumped back toward the main floor and the table got wedged in the stairwell.

There was another set of stairs near the back of the library they could use, but I had a little breathing room.

I rushed for the door to the outside balcony that runs half the length of the building.

It was locked.

A row of awning windows look out on the balcony. I pushed one open and scrambled over the sill. I landed on my hands and knees on the concrete floor of the balcony, jumped to my feet and dashed to the two-railed pipe balustrade that runs along the outer edge of the balcony. I looked down. It was at least a fifteen-foot drop to the alley below. I looked to the right. The bookmobile was backed up to the side door loading dock.

I heard glass shattering behind me.

No need to look back. I took five quick steps to the right, grabbed the top rail of the balustrade, and vaulted over it. I dropped about six feet to the roof of the bookmobile, landed on my butt, and bounced to the paved alley below. This time I landed on my feet. As soon as I touched down, I was on the move. I dashed down the alley and across the parking lot.

On the run, I dug in my pocket for the Porsche key, found it, and yelled, "Shit!"

Some clown had double-parked behind the Porsche, blocking my exit.

I kept running, hightailing it along the dirt path that led to Hartnell Street. I hit Hartnell and turned right. Before I'd run a dozen yards, I spotted a meter maid on the sidewalk in front of me, directly across the street from the post office. She was talking with a man who stood in the street, just behind a beat-up station wagon.

He was doing most of the talking and jabbing his finger at the rear bumper, punctuating his message with each jab.

My first instinct was to hit the brakes and reverse field. But a better instinct prevailed. I slowed to a normal walk. As I drew near the two, the man headed my way, pacing off a distance with deliberation. He bellowed each time his foot touched the pavement: "One! Two! Three!"

The meter maid walked beside him, staying on the sidewalk. The beef was probably about his not moving his car far enough from its previous parking space. I'd been ticketed for that in that same

24-minute green zone. Despite his righteous wrath, Mr. Angry Man was going to lose.

I strolled past them until I came abreast of the meter maid's three-wheel Cushman Truckster. It was double-parked, its motor running. I looked back at the two. Their backs were to me. Hell, I thought, I figured out how to steal a Porsche, this should be a piece of cake. I hopped into the Truckster, put it in drive, and pulled into traffic. I heard the shriek of brakes and a horn blaring. I glanced in the rearview mirror and saw a stalled delivery van behind me and the two cops from the library. They were running down the sidewalk, headed my way.

I drove along Hartnell for fifty feet and hung a left at Webster Street, cutting across the path of an oncoming mail truck. I accelerated into the turn, missing the truck by inches. The Cushman's center of gravity was high, and I thought for a moment I was going to ditch. But I let up a bit on the pedal and the vehicle leveled off. I goosed it again and continued on, gathering momentum as I sped—relatively speaking—down the hill. I held tight to the wheel, bouncing in and over every pothole and bump in my path.

The Truckster was no Porsche, but by the time I neared the Munras Avenue intersection at the bottom of the hill I was barreling along at twenty-something miles an hour. The traffic light at the intersection changed to red. I ignored it and stayed the course.

Coming from my right side, a black-and-yellow van from one of the hotels swerved to avoid me. It spun out into the center of the intersection, blocking traffic in all directions.

I heard a chorus of horns, but I didn't look back. I'd already zipped through the intersection and was headed for Abrego Street.

A guy in civilian clothes wouldn't get far in a meter maid's Truckster, but I'd put some distance between me and the two cops from the library. Brief respite. There'd soon be more cops, swarming after me like African killer bees.

I whipped into the parking lot of the Mid-Coast Savings and Loan and parked the Truckster between a van and the cement block wall at the end of the lot. The S&L occupied a two-story adobe-style building that took up half the block. I ducked into the alcove that faced Webster Street. A moment later a police car tore past, its cherry light flashing.

I felt safe for the moment, until a hand closed on my shoulder.

I spun about.

"Oh, sorry, Preston," a man said. "Didn't mean to startle you." He stuck out his hand. "Roger Newsome."

I noticed the merry play of blood vessels in his cheeks. The insurance man from the Commonwealth Club.

"Why, hello, Roger," I said and shook his hand.

Another police car streaked by, its siren wailing.

I raised my voice. "What a coincidence. I've been meaning to call you."

"Oh?"

"I'm not entirely happy with my present insurance carrier." I glanced at the key case in his other hand. "You wouldn't happen to have your car with you, would you? Mine's in the garage and I'm running late for an appointment."

Newsome beamed. He obviously wasn't up on the latest local news. He held up his keys and jingled them. "This must be your lucky day."

⁓

When we reached the crest of Monhollan Road, Newsome was still outlining a damn fine life-insurance program for me. I won't go into the details. Take my word for it—it was damn fine.

"Stop here!" I said, interrupting his spiel.

He looked bewildered; we were out in the middle of nowhere. But he eased his sedan to the side of the road and stopped.

I got out. "I'll walk the rest of the way. I need the exercise."

"But—"

"I'll call you Monday about that policy." I closed the door. It made a satisfying *thunk*. I gave him the Commonwealth wink.

Magic words. Magic wink. His brow smoothed out and he broke into a smile. He made a U-turn and headed back to town. I headed up the dirt road to Jacks Peak.

The cops hadn't found Ty's Bronco, but somebody had. The window on the driver's side was broken. I walked around the vehicle, checking for other damage.

"Oh-oh," I said when I got to the front. An Alpine hat was impaled on one of the steer horns. It brought back a vivid picture of the mushroom picker I'd almost creamed. I felt sheepish as I pulled the hat from the horn. Not because I'd nearly killed the guy—like matadors, wild mushroom hunters should know life is risky. It was because of my doubts about Scotty Dunbar.

If Scotty had brought the sheriff to Ty's house, it wasn't a plot against me. He probably hadn't recognized me last night. But even at eighty miles an hour, he'd have recognized Ty's steer horns.

Wires dangled from the empty slot on the Bronco's dashboard where the tape deck had been. The glove compartment was open and the registration, a road map, and a few other papers were scattered on the floor.

I took a crescent wrench and screwdriver from the tool kit and removed the steer horns from the grille. I stowed them on the back seat under a fleece car blanket. A step toward anonymity.

The key was under the floor mat where I'd left it. The Bronco started up on the first try and I backed out of the brush and onto the fire trail.

There were basically two ways to get to Nick Allred's place from there. I could take Highway 1 to the mouth of Carmel Valley and head out on Carmel Valley Road. Or I could head out Highway 68 toward Salinas and cross over Los Laureles Grade to Carmel Valley Road. On either route, though, there was a good chance I'd be spotted.

There was a less risky way than either of those, but it would take me through some rough terrain. It was a long shot, but what the hell—the odds had been screwed up ever since I'd gotten involved in this thing. I revved the engine and headed up the trail.

After I crested Jacks Peak, I followed the loop of a hiking trail for half a mile. It dipped and rose with the contours of the mountainside. A dozen feet wide and well-tended, the trail was designed more for Sunday strollers and horseback riders than for hard-core backpackers.

I stopped the Bronco at the bottom of a dip where a viewing area for hikers had been cleared. The small valley below was mostly grassland with clusters of scrub oak scattered here and there. On the other side of the valley a grass-covered slope led up to a bare ridge. I'd climbed to that ridge from the other side before, following a fire trail from Carmel Valley Road.

I shifted into low and swung off the trail. I headed downhill, skidding over shale, plowing through brush, and weaving my way through the trees. For the next ten minutes I was bouncing and sliding, gripping the wheel like a sea captain riding out a perfect storm. Not far from the bottom of the slope, the woods finally gave way to grassland.

Herky-jerky driving? Cam should eat her words. I was truly becoming the new Mario Andretti—with maybe a little Evel Knievel thrown in.

It was easier going up the other side, though I had an ugly moment of reflection as I plowed through a patch of poison oak. Once I'd eased over the ridge, it only took a minute to reach another fire trail, a relatively smooth dirt road.

It took another ten minutes to get to Carmel Valley Road. It was easy going, compared to what I'd just been through. It gave me a chance to think about Bingham.

Back at the Commonwealth Club, he'd called his stockbroker "Big Bull" and the guy had called him "Big Bear." At the time I didn't think of it in terms of the stock market; just more of that winky-wink stuff. Now it seemed obvious it wasn't a clubby nickname. Bingham played the bear market. And if he'd bought Mongoose stock short after Cobb was dead—but before anyone else knew about it—he'd have had the mother of all insiders' edges. He could clean up big time, and I bet myself he would.

That still left a batch of questions unanswered: What about the cop scene at his house? Had he told his housekeeper to call them? And why had he hidden me in a room where he knew I'd find a pistol? Was it a set-up? If so, why didn't he go through with it? He could have brought them right to the bedroom, but instead he let me get away. What the hell was his game plan?

I turned off Carmel Valley Road and onto the dirt road leading up to Nick's place. Unless I bumped heads with the law, I'd be at Nick's in twenty minutes.

CHAPTER 23

I followed the dirt road for a couple of miles and turned off it when I came to a field of dry grass. It looked like a smooth golden sea. It wasn't. The Bronco stagger-stepped through it, dipping into the gopher holes and bouncing over concealed rocks. A line of willows stretched across the far end of the field. A stream from Nick's pond flows there in the rainy season. Springs bubble up into the pond year-round, but there's not enough overflow to keep the stream flowing in summer. Now it was a dry arroyo.

A ridge on my left sloped down to the arroyo. Nick's place was just on the other side of it.

I drove down the embankment and followed the dry streambed, creeping along, bumping over the smooth stones that covered it. Now and then I'd hit a stretch of hard-packed sand and I could move a little faster. I stopped ten minutes later and turned off the engine. I left the Bronco in the streambed and climbed out of the arroyo. I was on the other side of the ridge now, about a quarter-mile from Nick's house.

My eyes stung from sweat and I wiped my face with my sleeve. It was almost six o'clock, and the sun was still baking the land. A twenty-five degree difference in temperature between Cachagua and the Monterey Peninsula isn't uncommon in the summer. It felt like the mid-nineties now.

I skirted the north side of the pasture and approached the rear of the house. Unless someone was looking out the kitchen window, they couldn't see me. When I was within a hundred feet of the house, I dropped into a crouch and began to run bent-legged through the tall grass. My face was coated with a combination of sweat and the chaff from the grass heads. When I reached the house, I pressed my back against the wall and wiped my face with my sleeve. I was sweating even more now. I dried my hands on my pants and took the pistol from my vest. I held it close to my shoulder, safety off, muzzle up, and edged toward the kitchen window. I trampled the herbs in Nick's garden as I moved and caught the scent of rosemary and mint.

I stopped just short of the window. I could hear music from inside the house—an old New Orleans rag. Had Nick returned?

I peeked through the kitchen window and could see through to the living room. Tiffany sat in the rocking chair by the coffee table, her back to the fireplace. She stared out the front window. She was wearing a tan poplin skirt and an aqua short-sleeved blouse. Despite the heat, she looked cool and lovely. I remembered how she'd looked in a white robe back at the Thomas Larkin Hotel two days ago. No. That was a doubly false memory. It was her twin sister, Jill—a lifetime ago.

I eased the kitchen door open and tiptoed into the house.

When I stepped into the living room, she gave a start. She sprang from the chair and rushed into my open arms.

"You got my message!" She buried her face in my chest. "I was so afraid something had happened to you."

"I'm okay," I said. "Have you heard from Bingham?"

She looked up. "Yes. He's on his way here."

"Here? When did you talk to him?"

"He called a little after I got here."

"You answered the phone?"

"I know I shouldn't have, Presto. But I thought it was you and—"

"Shh," I said. "It's all right." I put my hands on her shoulders and took a half step back. "I thought you were in L.A."

She shook her head. "No, I never left the area."

"Where?" I said. "I've been trying to get in touch with you."

"In Salinas," she said. "No one knows me there. I thought it was the safest place."

"Where in Salinas?"

"At a bed and breakfast place. I didn't want to risk going to a motel. You have to sign forms and use a credit card. I was afraid someone might find me."

"Which one?"

"I don't know. The something and something. A B&B name. It was run by an older couple, the Spelvins."

"Spelvin?" I said. "That's an uncommon name."

"Yes," she said. A little smile came to her lips. "I remembered, because that's the name of my massage therapist in L.A." Her smile faded. "But why are you asking me all these questions?"

"I've been worried about you," I said. "Come on. Sit down and I'll try to fill you in on what's been happening." I took her hand and led her over to the rocking chair. I pulled up a straight chair in front of her.

"Just a second," I said, "let me turn this off." I walked over to Nick's console. On the way, I took the magazine from the pistol, ejected the round from the chamber and stuck it into the magazine.

Nick's stereo setup looked like the control panel for a 747. I flicked some switches, pressed some buttons, twisted some knobs. The music played on.

"What's the matter?" Tiffany said.

"I'm low-tech," I said. "Give me a sec." I fiddled around a bit more. Finally, in the middle of a clarinet solo, the sound faded and died.

I went back and sat down in the chair in front of her. I held the pistol up in front of me to catch the light coming through the window. I pulled back the slide and blew into the open chamber. I closed it, slid a magazine into the pistol, and racked the slide again. I set it on the coffee table and took her hands in mine.

"It's Bingham," I said.

"Bingham?"

"Cobb's killer. Your sister's killer. The attempts on my life."

She shook her head. "But I talked with him … I told him everything—"

She pulled her hands free and let them fall into her lap. The tears started again. She sniffed, took a tissue from the box on the coffee table, and dabbed at her nose. "Oh, Presto, I put your life in danger. I didn't know what to do, and—Oh, my god! He's on his way here!" She brought her hands to her face and covered her mouth with them.

"It's okay," I said. "Everything going to be all right."

"It's all my fault, Presto. I'm to blame for everything. I'm so sorry."

She picked up the pistol.

"Careful," I said, "the safety's off."

She nodded, and the corners of her mouth turned up in a smile. She looked toward the bedroom. "Come on out," she said. "I've got his gun."

⌇

Foster Bingham stepped into the room. He was in shirtsleeves, but he still wore the blue necktie with the little red golf clubs on it. He cradled one of Nick's shotguns in his arms.

"Well done, Jill," he said to the young woman with the gun.

"Easy as pie," she said. "Mr. Kane isn't the sharpest knife in the drawer."

"Doesn't seem so, does it?" Bingham said. His winning smile was in full flower.

CHAPTER 24

"All that business at the Larkin Hotel," I said to Bingham, "it had nothing to do with this."

"That's right," Bingham said. "It was just some of Jerry Racker's hi-jinks—an offshoot of his dungeons-and-dragons mentality. You met him. You know what I mean."

I did.

"He thought something was fishy about the deal," Bingham said, "and he wanted more information."

"There must have been an easier way to get it."

"He's a jerk," Bingham said. "And, believe it or not, Cobb was a bigger jerk. That's why it was such a delightful situation for a while. The amount of money to be made was considerable."

"And Cobb backed out."

"Cobb was as sneaky as Racker. His Carmel house was wired. He intercepted a phone call between Racker and Jill and discovered that the two had worked out the auction scam and that I had set it up."

"I thought it was your lawyer friend in Boston."

"No, Lew thought the auction was legitimate, and so did Nadine."

"You were using them both."

"No harm, no foul. Lew wouldn't be involved and Nadine would make out like a bandit. But when Cobb got wise, he booted Jill out and came to *Rancho de los Lobos* and threatened me with a lawsuit. I told him we could go ahead with the auction, but I'd rig it so Racker would be the sucker, not him. I'd cut off the bidding when it looked like Racker wouldn't go any higher."

"But Racker could still back out."

"Of course. But Cobb had a good case against me, and by then I realized I had to protect myself. If he went along with the plan, his case against me would become moot."

"Cobb may have been a creep, but he wasn't a moron. What made you think he'd fall for it?"

"It was a long shot, but I was in desperate straits. I tried to reason with him, but things got heated. Push came to shove—literally. In the course of the scuffle, he slipped and hit his head on my hearth. I tried to revive him, but that wasn't to be."

I didn't bother mentioning that the *Mercury News* had reported the cause of death was strangulation.

"How did he end up in Monterey Bay?"

"When I went to put his body in the trunk of his car, his wetsuit was in it. I brought him back to the house and put it on him. Believe me," he said, "it isn't easy to dress a corpse in a wetsuit."

"I'll take your word for it," I said.

"That night I dumped him near Lovers Point and left his car on a side street. The tide did the rest. Jill had followed me there and she brought me back home."

"And the next day you sold your Mongoose stock before news of Cobb's could death get out"

He shrugged. "It was bound to plummet. For a while after Cobb's death I could have sold the Windsor Star to Racker without an auction. But I decided it would raise suspicions. By the time you got to the Larkin Hotel, the Star was irrelevant. Nadine didn't know

Cobb was dead yet, but she soon would. I decided to cut my losses, and I had Damon clean things up."

"By slugging me."

"Why not? If you made a fuss, we could attribute it all to Racker. And who'd believe your story, anyway?"

"Thanks," I said. "So, throughout our lunch, you were just bull-shitting me."

He tilted his head back and raised his eyes, as though the crude expression pained him. He shrugged. "In a word—yes."

"You were just killing time—and having Tiffany killed.

"She was a liability," Bingham said. "She knew too much and we had to rein her in."

If I were wearing a hat, I'd have tipped it to Bingham. "Rein her in" was a brilliant euphemism for murder, even for a lawyer.

"You sent the albino to my house to kill her and plant cocaine there."

"The albino?" Bingham smiled. "His name was Gregory, actual-ly."

"And the police would put her murder on me."

"They would have, if your neighbor hadn't seen Gregory leaving."

"And you sent him to kill me at Cobb's beach house."

"Not entirely my plan. It was actually a favor for Gregory. You'd made life very stressful for him. You thwarted him when he and Damon visited you in Pacific Grove. And the Cachagua business was even more distressing for him. He was very fond of Damon. It was his idea, actually, to lure you to the beach house. He had special plans for you. Something that might look like you'd double-crossed a drug cartel. You were very fortunate to avoid that, though I can't imagine how you did it."

"I guess it was my lucky day," I said.

Bingham chuckled.

"Another thing," I said. "Where did you get the helicopter?"

"From an oilman in South County, a client," Bingham said. "I help him with land projects in San Ardo. He helps me with some of my projects."

"What a noble philosophy," I said. "One hand helping the other."

I turned to Jill. "You were the one in rehab in L.A."

"That's right."

"And the second time, in rehab up here."

"Grow up," she said. "There wasn't a second time. That was a story. I was putting you on."

"About the pearl necklace, too."

That struck a nerve. She frowned and pressed her lips together as though blotting lipstick. "There was a pearl necklace," she said. "Our aunt let us play dress-up one day, and Tiffany got to wear her pearls. I got to wear her crummy Jackie Kennedy pillbox hat. When we were done playing, Auntie Dear took them back. She said that when we grew up, Tiffany could have the pearls and I could have the stupid hat."

"So you stole the pearls."

She made an ugly laughing sound. "I did. And I flushed them down the toilet."

"You were the designated bad girl growing up and Tiffany was Miss Innocent. And you continued to play those roles to the end."

"Jesus," she said, "you are *so* dense. Tiffany was in on this from the start. She got Racker into the bidding game."

"So why did you tell me about Cahill? Didn't you realize he'd tell me what was really going on?"

She shook her head. "You really are amazing. It was to get you away from your friend Nick's place, so *I* could get away from there. I didn't want to be around when the helicopter showed up. After that, it wouldn't make any difference what Cahill told you."

I guessed it wouldn't have, if I hadn't been outside when the helicopter arrived.

I turned to Bingham. "I still don't know what you had in mind when I showed up at Los Lobos. I knew you had the maid call the police, but I don't know why you didn't have them arrest me."

Bingham shook his head. "You've got an active imagination, Preston. I didn't have Anna call the police. It actually *was* a surprise visit. They were there to solicit my annual donation to the Police Athletic League. I've been on the board for the last eight years. I didn't want them to see you, of course, because I had other plans for you." He chuckled. "But your stealing my pistol and their police car was pure serendipity. They thought you'd come to kill me. I protested, but they insisted that was the case. And now it's come to this."

He smiled. "As Shakespeare wrote: 'Oh what a tangled web we weave, when first we practice to deceive.'"

"Sir Walter Scott."

"Huh?"

"That's who wrote it."

He frowned. "Are you sure about that? I'll have to check it out."

"You do that," I said. "But first, tell me why you got into this mess? You could have pulled out of it, even after Cobb's death. How could anyone prove it wasn't an accident? But you dug yourself in deeper when you unloaded your Mongoose stock."

"A chance I had to take," Bingham said. "I'd recently made some unfortunate financial decisions, took some hard hits. I hoped the Windsor Star sale would level the playing field again. When Cobb pulled out, that opportunity was lost. But his death presented another opportunity. I actually made money on selling my Mongoose stock, and there's a very good chance that since Cobb is no longer competing with his hated ex-partner, my Cobra stock is bound to rise."

I said, "'Once the dog was dead, there was no reason not to eat it.'" It was a quote from an AP story that came over the wire when I was working at the *Eagle*. It was about a homeless man who'd been busted in L.A. for cooking and eating a dead dog he'd found in an alley. The words were those of his lawyer.

I doubt Bingham knew what I was referring to specifically, but he caught the gist of it. I guess lawyers are trained to think that way.

"Makes sense," Bingham said. "If you get a lemon, make lemonade. Once this thing got in motion, there was no reason not to make the best of it." He smiled. "It assumed a life of its own."

"You give fate too much credit, Bingham. This thing grew out of your trying to screw Cobb out of money with the bidding scam."

"That was legal," he said.

"That's what the lawyer said about eating the dog. What about having Tiffany killed? Any thoughts on that, attorney?"

He swiped me across the head with the pistol, right where Scriven had hit me earlier. It hurt like a bastard. But I wasn't letting up.

"Sooner or later," I said, "somebody's going to put the pieces together."

"Let me tell you a story," he said. "Two friends go hiking together and come across a grizzly bear's paw prints. One of them takes a pair of running shoes from his pack. The other one says, 'That's foolish. Even with running shoes you can't outrun a grizzly bear.' The first man says, 'I don't have to. I just have to outrun *you.*'"

He smiled. "I don't have to prove my innocence. I just have to establish your guilt."

I didn't reply.

We all turned to the front window at the sound of a car approaching. Dust rose in the distance, and moments later a blue Camaro barreled into the yard and skidded to a halt.

"I told them you'd be surrendering," Bingham said. "I insisted you were innocent. But for some reason, they aren't convinced."

The door to the Camaro opened and Raymond Scriven stepped out. He was wearing a black-and-orange San Francisco Giants T-shirt. I'd never seen him in civilian clothes before, but I had no trouble recognizing him. His shark-fin beak alone set him off from the normal run of humanity. He leaned into the car and came out with a police utility belt. He strapped it on and headed toward us.

"So," I said to Bingham, "you shoot Scriven with your pistol—which they think I stole from you. And then you shoot me with Scriven's pistol."

He gave me a Commonwealth Club wink. "Everybody who saw the front page of the *Eagle* knows how you feel about Scriven. I can see the editorials. They'll say it was inevitable."

Jill went to the door and opened it for Scriven. He stepped inside and nodded to Bingham. "Thanks for the tip, sir."

"You're alone?"

"Back-up's on the way." He gestured out the doorway. In the distance another cloud of dust was rising. "But I'll make this bust on my own."

He turned to me and grinned. He took his handcuffs from his belt and stepped toward me. "Kane," he said, "I *will* Miranda you this time. 'You have the absolute right to remain silent. Anything you say can, and will, be used against you in a court of law. You have the right to consult with an attorney—'"

"No need for that," Bingham said.

Scriven turned to him.

Bingham set the shotgun down and picked up the pistol. He aimed it at Scriven's chest.

Scriven's face twisted into a scowl. "What the fuck is this?"

"Don't worry," I said. "It's not loaded."

Bingham gave me a pained look. "Oh for God's sake, Preston."

"It's a fact, Bingham," I said. "You don't think I'd give Jill a loaded gun when I knew she was lying, do you?"

Bingham smiled. "But you didn't know she was lying when you gave it to her. And you thought she was sweet Tiffany."

"No, Bingham. I knew she was lying. And I've suspected she was Jill for a while now."

"I doubt that."

"She confirmed it when I asked her about the bed and breakfast where she'd stayed in Salinas. She said it was run by an older couple—the Spelvins. Come on, Bingham—Spelvins? Do you know anybody named Spelvin? It's a name actors use when they don't want their real names listed. It's an old theatrical tradition. One every actor is familiar with."

Bingham raised an eyebrow.

I nodded toward Jill. "Am I right?"

She shrugged. "Yeah."

Bingham tilted the pistol and looked at it.

"Bingham," I said, "there are no bullets in the gun. You had a full magazine in it and an empty one in the drawer." I pulled the full magazine from my side pocket and snapped a round out onto the floor. "I switched them."

"I don't believe you," he said. He turned to Scriven and pointed the pistol at him again.

Scriven believed me. He dropped the handcuffs to the floor and reached for his own pistol.

Bingham's pistol went click, and Scriven's right hand came up with his pistol in it. The roar from the Glock 17 rocked the room. Four rounds ripped into Bingham's chest and slammed him back-wards across the room. For the blink of an eye he looked like a display specimen pinned to the wall. And then he slid to the floor.

There was no need to check his pulse.

Scriven spun my way. The pistol hand dangled at his side now. He raised the other hand and jabbed his finger at me several times.

I thought of a rooster pecking at corn.

"I ought to shoot you now," he said.

"Do it!" Jill said. She stared at him, nodding, coaxing him to act. Scriven looked at her, his mouth half open.

"Do it!" she said. "Shoot him! I won't tell!"

They stared into each other's eyes, and I sensed a rapport be-tween them—a meeting of bad karmas.

"He wouldn't dare shoot me," I said.

His jaw clenched so tightly the muscles stood out at the sides. We were locked eye-to-eye. After a moment, his shoulders slumped and his hand dropped to his side.

"Asshole," he said. He bent down and picked up the handcuffs.

"Turn around and put your hands behind your back!"

I did as he said, bracing myself for a blow. It never came. He clapped the cuffs on me and stepped back.

"I'm not done with you," he said. It was a half-hearted move to save face, but I guess it was the best he could muster.

He scooped up the shotgun and Bingham's empty .45. He looked over at Bingham's body with a blank expression, as though it had nothing to do with him. Then he turned and headed out toward the sheriff's car, which had just come to a stop in the driveway.

"It's okay!" he shouted, "I've got it under control!"

As soon as he was outside, Jill rushed to my side. She clutched my arm. "Don't involve me," she said. "They don't have anything on me. If you don't talk, there's no problem."

"No problem?"

"You don't have to bring me into this. I didn't do anything. I was misled by Binx, but I never did any harm."

"Jill," I said, "you set me up to be murdered. You set Scriven up, too. You share the responsibility for your own sister's death. And you've been in tight with Bingham from the start."

She smiled and shook her head. When she spoke, her voice was gentle and steady. She sounded like a kindergarten teacher reassuring an anxious child. "No, dear, don't you see? It wasn't my fault. I didn't do anything wrong. It was Jill. She's the one who should be punished. She's the bad one."

I didn't say anything. Was this another snow job? I looked her in the eye and I couldn't tell whether she was acting or not. I honestly couldn't say.

⸻

Scriven wanted to keep the handcuffs on me, but his superior overrode him. When the cuffs were off me, I went over to Nick's console and turned off the tape recorder.

I'd have some tall explaining to do when Nick got back. I'd recorded over one of his traditional jazz tapes.

I rewound the reel and gave it to one of the deputies. "You'd better protect this," I said. "It's all on there. Everything. It'll even vindicate Scriven for shooting Bingham."

I handed it to him and a flash of light filled the room. I turned to the doorway.

Scotty Dunbar stood there, his camera pressed to his face.

I wasn't surprised.

CHAPTER 25

Nick, Cam, Ty and I celebrated with a dinner at Fandango in downtown Pacific Grove. My treat, thanks to Nadine Stoughton. Nick had filled her in on what happened, and she'd sent me a generous bonus check for my efforts. In the note that accompanied it, she mentioned that the publicity surrounding the Windsor Star had greatly increased its value.

A few days before our dinner, Nick and I had gone up to Carver's Ridge and found his pistol. There was no trace of Damon or his rifle. Maybe Gregory had come back for them. I don't know where they might be now and have no interest in knowing.

There was no trace of the rattlesnake I shot either. We figure a vulture or some other carrion-eater had carried it off. The subject came up at dinner and Nick teased me about exaggerating the snake's size."

"I don't doubt him," Cam said, "I've heard anacondas can reach thirty feet." She gave me a patronizing look. "Do you think that's what it was, Presto?"

The little vixen hadn't lost her edge in Chicago.

Boy, it was great to see her again.

I apologized again to Nick for ruining his binoculars and recording over his music tape. He said, "Forget it. I guess it was for a good cause."

I nodded. The tape saved my ass. What better cause?

The tape might help Jill Swift, too. She sounded like a cold-hearted killer early on. But when she shifted into Tiffany mode, she was convincing. Her lawyers could use that at her trial. I'm sure they could dig up a psychiatrist or two to diagnose her as a multiple-personality victim.

Was she? A part of me wanted to think so. Being tricked by a madwoman stung less than being made a fool of by an evil one. But another part of me had to accept her own self-description: She was a first-class actress.

The tape certainly helped Scriven. Internal Affairs felt it justified his using deadly force. In fact, he's up for a commendation. The tape indicated he'd fired just as Bingham was pulling down on him. I could have told them about the look in his eye when he realized Bingham's gun was empty. But why bother? They wouldn't believe me.

I didn't make a big thing out of the threat he'd made to me, and the cops didn't make a big thing out of the various vehicles I'd commandeered. We were even up. Adam Spaeder—Nick's lawyer pal—was working it out with the insurance companies to pay for damage to Nick's, Ty's, and the Porsche driver's cars. I never did find out what happened to my car. Maybe Jill had sold it—or even parked it on the street with the key in it. No great loss. Certainly not as great as the loss of my $15 recliner.

The dinner was both a celebration and a reunion. I'd talked with Cam on the phone a few times since her return, but this was the first time we'd gotten together. I thought it might be easier to have Nick and Ty along as a buffer. Frankly, I was nervous.

I didn't know if we could pick up where we left off—or if she even wanted to. She was back in the area for sure. She'd nixed a return to local TV, but the Monterey Institute of International Studies was looking for someone with a strong background in communications. After a short interview, they offered her the job and she accepted. She announced the news at our dinner.

Ty—as is his custom—cut to the chase. "Cam," he said, "was it the potent allure of Mr. Kane that brought you back to our little piece of heaven?"

She didn't skip a beat. "What cinched it, Ty, was the intense desire to never freeze my ass off in another Chicago winter."

Salty Cam.

—⁓—

It was a rare balmy night in Pacific Grove, and after dinner Cam and I walked from the restaurant to her place on Sunset Drive. She invited me in for coffee and we sat on the couch with the lights out, looking out at the ocean, and reminiscing. Before long we were holding hands. I remembered how I loved the scent of her hair and the unaffected way she laughed when she was happy. A host of memories came flooding back.

I tried to act nonchalant when I told her that Nick had offered me the use of his Foresta cabin anytime he wasn't using it. "In fact," I said, "we could go up there this weekend … if you're interested."

She hesitated and I wondered if I'd blown it. Was I pressing too hard?

"Okay," she said. "But on one condition."

Oh well, I thought, if it's separate beds, so be it.

"What's the condition?"

She gave me the eagle eye and said, "I drive."

JEFFREY WHITMORE

Writing as Sterling Johnson, Pacific Grove author Jeffrey Whitmore has written the novel *Dangerous Knaves* and the St Martin's Press best selling humor book *English as a Second F*cking Language* ("Great f*cking book!"—Steven King).

As Prescott Hill, he's written more than 30 hi-lo books for young readers. Under his own name, his fiction has appeared in Rod Serling's *Twilight Zone Magazine* and the online magazines *Deep Outside SFFH* and *Sour Grapes*. His work also appears in *Life in Pacific Grove, California Book 2: Deeper Connections*. His 55-word (including title) short story "Bedtime Story" ("Rather wonderful." *Introduction to Narrative*, Cambridge University Press) is featured in *World's Shortest Stories*(Running Press) and numerous other publications.

Lovers Point Cove, Pacific Grove, California.
16"x20" oil painting by Carmel artist Kevin Milligan.
Courtesy of Patricia Hamilton.